'We'd be..h reluctan......

Although sh......................Dan to make love to her, Trudi was reluctant to start an affair with him so soon. It would mean having to tell him a lot more about herself—a whole lot more—and after the remarks he'd made earlier about disapproving of surrogacy, she just couldn't face it right now.

She was relieved that he appeared not to want to rush into an affair.

He cupped her face in his hand. 'From the moment I first saw you I knew you were someone special. I'm not going to spoil it by rushing things. Something as good as this needs to be taken slowly. Do you feel the same?'

Trudi nodded. Dan was a dream come true, a man she could fall madly in love with—if she hadn't done so already. But her joy in knowing him was tempered by the fact that she feared there could never be a future for them. If he disapproved so strongly about surrogacy, which was how it had very much sounded, how on earth was she ever going to be able to tell him the truth about Grace and her conception?

Barbara Hart was born in Lancashire and educated at a convent in Wales. At twenty-one she moved to New York, where she worked as an advertising copywriter. After two years in the USA she returned to England, where she became a television press officer in charge of publicising a top soap opera and a leading current affairs programme. She gave up her job to write novels. She lives in Cheshire and is married to a solicitor. They have two grown-up sons.

Recent titles by the same author:

HER FATHER'S DAUGHTER

A FATHER FOR HER CHILD

BY
BARBARA HART

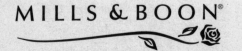

MILLS & BOON®

To Mary O'Brien
friend and medical advisor

First published in Great Britain 2001
Harlequin Mills & Boon Limited,
Eton House, 18-24 Paradise Road, Richmond, Surrey TW9 1SR

© Barbara Hart 2001

ISBN 0 263 82654 6

Set in Times Roman 10½ on 12 pt.
03-0301-44153

Printed and bound in Spain
by Litografia Rosés, S.A., Barcelona

CHAPTER ONE

PERCHED on a kitchen stool, Trudi experienced another contraction. She held her bump and rocked gently backwards and forwards in a primitive attempt to ease the pain. And then another one came. A much stronger one this time—so strong it made her gasp. This baby was definitely on the way.

This baby. This baby she'd carried for nine months. The baby she'd tried to distance herself from and attempted to forget about in her day-to-day life. And for nearly seven months she'd succeeded in doing just that. It had only been a couple of months ago that she'd begun to look the slightest bit pregnant. She was tall—five feet eight—and slim, and the baby had seemed to tuck itself in so neatly that until a few weeks ago she'd still been able to wear her normal clothes. Then wham! In the final weeks her stomach had ballooned and she'd looked just as pregnant as all the other mums-to-be at the antenatal clinic.

It had been then, especially at the times when the baby had kicked and moved around and had generally made its presence felt that she'd become more and more attached to this little life inside her. It had been then that Annie's words had come back to haunt her. Annie, who used to be Trudi's best friend.

'How can you do it, Trudi? How *can* you give your baby away?'

The two girls were in the hospital restaurant, having a coffee-break. Trudi had just told her friend that she was having a baby for her sister. Annie's reaction made Trudi regret she'd ever told her. The things Annie said that day made Trudi decide she would leave Mayside General as soon as she could and get a new job in another hospital as far away from her home town as possible.

'Giving your baby away!' repeated Annie incredulously.

'I won't be just giving my baby away,' protested Trudi. 'I've gone in for this with my eyes wide open, so I'm well prepared—emotionally and psychologically. My sister and brother-in-law were absolutely desperate for a baby. I was really very worried that they might get ill with the depression they were suffering. My sister in particular.'

Annie said nothing. She wasn't convinced.

'I mean, can you imagine, Annie, what it must be like at thirty years of age, being told you had to have a hysterectomy? After trying unsuccessfully for years to have a baby? All the fertility treatments that were going? And then finally losing your womb? Can you imagine what that does to your sanity?'

'I know all that, Trudi. I was just as upset as you were when you told me about Jane's operation last year.'

'Don't be silly, Annie,' retorted Trudi. 'You couldn't possibly be as upset as I was! She's my sister, not yours. You haven't even got a sister. You have no idea how close we are, my sister and I. We'd do anything for each other.'

'I still think having a baby for someone else, no

matter how close you are, is taking things a bit too far,' said Annie stubbornly. 'It's unnatural. You'll never be able to give the baby up after you've given birth. I know lots of people do it—surrogacy. I've read all about it in the tabloids. But I never thought you'd do it. In fact, I don't think you *will* do it. I think you'll keep the baby because you'll never be able to give it up!'

'I'm sorry I told you.' Trudi was feeling sick. Not sick with the pregnancy which was still in its very early days. But the way Annie had reacted to her news had turned her stomach. If this was the way her best friend was going to react to the news, what about everyone else? All her other friends and colleagues?

There wouldn't be much of a problem with family as Trudi and her sister Jane had very few living relatives, just a few distant cousins. The two sisters had been sent away to boarding school when they were very young. Their titled parents had told them it would be 'a lot of fun'. What they'd really meant, no doubt, had been that it would be a lot more fun for them because, with their children out of the way for most of the year, they could carry on with their self-centred, extravagant lifestyle.

Their parents had been killed in a boating accident when the girls had barely left boarding school. It had happened just as their father had been about to be declared bankrupt and had probably been intended as a final luxury holiday before the bailiffs moved in. As well as the tragedy of losing both parents, the Honourable Jane and the Honourable Trudi Younghouse had had to get jobs pretty quickly in order to support themselves, having found they'd had very little to live on from their debt-ridden inheritance. In their adversity they'd become even closer.

'It still sounds a very strange thing to do,' persisted Annie. 'To have a baby and just hand it over to someone else. It must be the worst thing in the world. Oh, and by the way, who's the father of this baby?'

'My brother-in-law, Rob. And before you ask, we used a special syringe!'

Trudi walked away before Annie could see the tears that had suddenly welled up in her eyes.

And now here she was, seven months later, clutching her stomach and wondering if Annie's prediction was going to come true. *You'll never be able to give it up!* Her words had come back to haunt Trudi in the past two months. Would she be able to give up this baby? Hand it over to her desperate sister? Well, the way the contractions were progressing, she was going to be finding out pretty soon.

She picked up the phone and rang her sister's number. Jane had wanted to take Trudi into hospital and wait with her and watch the baby being born. The phone rang four times then her sister's answerphone came on.

'Damn,' muttered Trudi through gritted teeth as the pains came with increasing strength and regularity. 'Jane, it's Trudi here. It's four o'clock in the afternoon and I'm pretty sure the baby's coming. I'll have to ring for an ambulance as you're not at home. See you and Rob at the hospital.'

*   *   *

On a scale of one to ten, Trudi reckoned the birth came about number six. It wasn't the worst birth she'd imagined it could be—but neither was it a piece of cake. One of the things that made it worse was the fact that Jane didn't seem to have got the message. Trudi was sure that her sister would have come flying round at speed the moment she knew the baby—'her' baby—was about to be born. She'd been so keen to be there that Trudi just couldn't understand why she hadn't arrived during the hours of labour which had seemed to go on for an eternity.

When she was wheeled into the delivery room, Trudi kept asking, 'Has my sister arrived yet? Please, page the waiting area in case she's there.'

But she wasn't there, the midwife kept telling her. 'We'll bring her up the moment she comes. Now, when I say push, give it all you've got.'

Just when Trudi thought the baby would never be born, she gave one final push and her little daughter slithered into the world and was placed in her arms. It was the most exquisite moment of her life as she looked at the tiny red body lying on her breast.

At that instant, the greatest surge of love she'd ever known rushed from her heart into this baby. It must be hormones, she thought as she blinked away tears of…what? Joy? Happiness? Sadness? Despair? This was the baby she must not get attached to. This is the daughter she would have to think of, always, as a niece. It was like being hit with a blunt instrument, so strong were the emotions that filled her, now that she had the baby on her breast, in her arms. Annie's words rang in her ears. *You'll never be able to give it up!*

'Oh, you're crying, love,' said the kindly midwife. 'Is it because you wanted a boy? Never mind, you can have a boy next time. I've got three boys and I'd love a little girl like yours.'

Trudi shook her head. 'We wanted a girl. My sister and I.'

'And what about the baby's father?' asked the midwife, slightly confused. 'Did he want a girl, too?'

'Oh, yes,' said Trudi, kissing the halo of tiny red hair on the baby's head. 'Rob wanted a daughter. He'll be delighted.'

The young doctor who'd attended the birth took the baby gently from Trudi.

'I'll just give her a quick check-up, see that she's OK,' he said.

Trudi was aware of urgent voices outside the delivery theatre. The midwife was called out. Trudi saw the flash of a blue uniform. Two blue uniforms, a policeman and a policewoman. She heard her name mentioned. A terrible dread filled her.

'What is it?' she said, trying to sit up.

'It's all right,' said the doctor. 'Just relax there for a little while. You've done all the hard work now and your baby is as fit as a fiddle. Nothing to worry about at all.'

The midwife came back into the theatre, fixed expression on her face. She murmured something to the doctor, then turned to Trudi.

'There's been a bit of bad news about your sister, dear.'

'Jane? Something's happened to Jane?'

'I'm afraid so. But you're not to get yourself upset.

There's been a motor accident. On the way to the hospital, apparently.'

'Accident? And how are they? How are Jane and Rob?'

'Not good.' The midwife was struggling with her conscience. How could she tell this young woman who'd just had a baby that her sister and brother-in-law had been killed in a road accident?

'How bad are they?' asked Trudi, her heart thumping.

'It's as bad as it can be,' said the midwife, taking Trudi's hand gently in hers. 'They were both killed instantly, I'm afraid, not more than half a mile from here.'

Dan Donovan, the newly appointed paediatric cardiologist at Highfield Hospital, was a contented man. His life plan was well on target. Here he was in a top medical job in a major children's hospital and he was still two weeks off his thirty-fifth birthday.

Not bad for a working-class boy!

He couldn't remember a time when he hadn't been fired with an ambition to succeed. While his schoolmates had been secretly smoking behind the bike sheds, Dan had been secretly sneaking home with stacks of library books to supplement the meagre supply of school textbooks. He'd kept his studying a secret from his mates because no self-respecting Yorkshire schoolboy wanted to be labelled a swot.

His parents were great. An inspiration. Between them they'd worked all the hours they'd possibly been able to, his dad doing long shifts in a carpet factory, his mam working evenings, stocking supermarket shelves, in order to give their children a better chance in life. They had been so proud when he'd gone to university and had then become a doctor. His sister, Clare, was also in the medical profession. She was a senior nurse, working at Highfield Hospital. That was, between having babies. Three children in four years meant she'd been on almost continuous maternity leave. Now that the youngest was six months old, Clare was taking advantage of the marvellous crèche facilities at the hospital and going back to work part time.

The buzz of the intercom jerked Dan out of his reverie. That was the signal for his first patient.

The door was opened by a nurse who brought in a stack of patient files.

'Grace Younghouse is the first one,' she said. 'Shall I call her in?'

'Yes please, Nurse.' Dan flicked open the top file as the nurse directed the mother and baby to the chairs at the side of Dan's desk. He glanced up, smiling a welcome.

Trudi looked into the ruggedly handsome face of the paediatrician. He had short dark hair, big brown eyes and powerful-looking shoulders.

'Hello, Mrs Younghouse,' said Dan. 'Just give me a moment to read through Grace's file.'

His voice was reassuringly warm with an attractive Northern bluntness to it—probably Lancashire or Yorkshire, Trudi guessed.

Dan noted that the file was very thin, hardly anything in it at all except the form filled in by the baby's mother and a short letter from her GP.

'Something about a heart murmur? Is that right?'

he asked, looking up from his desk, this time paying more attention to the young woman sitting in front of him. He registered how pretty she was, with tousled auburn hair and a creamy skin with just a dusting of freckles. She seemed nervous, her face tight with anxiety. He recognised that look in so many parents when they believed, rightly or wrongly, that there was something seriously the matter with their child.

Trudi held baby Grace close to her as she explained the situation.

'Yesterday I took the baby to the clinic for a check-up and a young doctor said he thought she might have a heart murmur.' Tears filled her eyes. 'I'm so scared something could be seriously wrong with her.'

The upper-class accent caught him unawares. Her well-spoken accent and softly modulated tones had the effect of making him go hot under the collar. He found that kind of voice very sexy. It reminded him of…well, best not to think about that now. He cleared his throat before speaking.

'I'm sure you're worrying for nothing,' he said as evenly as he could, his own Yorkshire accent becoming more pronounced. 'Murmurs are often mistakenly diagnosed in young babies, and even if there is one, it doesn't necessarily mean there's a problem. It's something that could right itself.'

Dan stood up and went over to the sink to wash his hands in preparation for the examination. He was tall, noticed Trudi, well over six feet, with narrow hips and long legs.

'Did you say yesterday?' he queried. 'The Health Service is moving quicker than I thought!'

'Well, actually, I pulled a few strings to get to see you as quickly as possible,' admitted Trudi.

'I can imagine,' replied Dan, speaking his thoughts out loud. Pulling a few strings at board level, no doubt. With an accent like that she was probably on cocktail-party terms with everyone of any importance. The upper classes had their own, very effective form of networking. The old school tie was still very much in evidence, even in these more egalitarian days. Not that he'd got a chip on his shoulder! Or was prejudiced in any way! He took people as he found them.

'Can you?' She was confused, but continued to explain. 'You see, I'm a nurse and I'd been doing agency work before Grace was born and I worked here for a couple of months. So yesterday, when I got this terrible shock, I just rang a friend here at Highfield and she managed to fit me in straight away.'

'I see,' said Dan, the first of his preconceptions about her blown away. So she works, does she? he thought. Well, there's a surprise.

He looked at her again, critically. She was quite something—gorgeous hair, adorable face and terrific legs. He couldn't see what her breasts looked like as she was holding the baby very close to her. He shook himself out of his fantasising.

'Now, let's have a look at the patient,' he said, reaching his hand out to touch the baby gently on the cheek. 'How old is she?'

'Four months. Will you examine her on my knee

or should I lay her over there?' asked Trudi, indicating the examination table.

'If she's a calm baby I'd prefer to examine her on the table,' said Dan. 'The supine position gives me better access to the apex of the heart.' He stood over the baby, looking at her angelic little face. 'You seem to be a very tranquil little girl. Not a cry-baby at all,' said Dan to Grace, who gave him a beatific smile in response.

Trudi laid her on the cushioned table and removed her tiny T-shirt. Dan placed the warmed stethoscope on her chest and listened to the familiar lub-dub sound of the infant's heart. Then he put a gentle hand on the baby's chest to feel the rise and fall of the chest wall, noting the depth, rhythm and breath sounds as he counted the beats.

When he'd finished the examination he told Trudi to put the T-shirt back on Grace and indicated that they should both take a seat again. Trudi's own heart was beating like mad in the short time between the examination and hearing the diagnosis.

'I'll put your mind at rest straight away,' he said, smiling broadly. 'I couldn't detect anything abnormal in your baby's heartbeat.'

Trudi grinned back at him in hysterical relief. She started to laugh.

'Oh, I can't tell you how that makes me feel! That's the best news I've ever had in my life!'

Trudi's grin lit up her entire face, transforming a pale, serious young woman into a beauty with shining eyes and glowing skin. Dan was mesmerised. He'd never seen such a change come over anyone so quickly, or so appealingly. Even the baby startled chuckling as she picked up her mother's happy mood.

Dan, who in other circumstances would have been anxious to move his list on quickly, felt himself wanting to detain this young woman for a minute or two longer than necessary.

'So, you worked here as a nurse?' he quizzed.

'I did before Grace was born, yes.' Trudi just couldn't stop grinning, she felt so happy and relieved. And she couldn't stop chattering either. Quite unlike herself in recent months, clamming up whenever anyone had started to ask personal questions. 'I don't remember you being here then,' she added. 'But, of course, it's a huge hospital.'

'I've only just started here. I was at a London hospital until recently,' replied Dan. 'This is my first week.' His smile revealed a flash of gleaming white teeth in dazzling contrast to his tanned face and dark hair.

'That explains why I didn't see you, then.' What an inane thing to say, thought Trudi, still firmly settled into the chair and not wanting to make the first move to leave.

'And will you be coming back after your maternity leave?' he quizzed further. Why am I being so nosy? thought Dan, unable to stop himself from this line of questioning.

'Yes,' she replied, noting the way his eyebrows lifted slightly when she answered in the affirmative.

'And when will that be?'

'In about eight weeks, I should think,' said Trudi, who hadn't answered so many personal questions in months—not since her conversation with her former

best friend Annie. Personal questions were something she now avoided like the plague. Yet she didn't
seem to mind this man asking her all sorts of things.
She was also volunteering information into the bargain!

'I've managed to get Grace into the hospital crèche
when she's six months old. I believe it's really good.
That's the main reason I'm getting a job at Highfield,
so that I can be close to her.'

'My sister uses the crèche,' said Dan. 'You might
come across her. Her name's Clare and she now
works part time as a phlebotomist, collecting the
blood samples. She was a senior ward sister, but now
she has the children she only wants a part-time job.
I expect you'll be the same.'

'No, I shall be coming back full time,' said Trudi.
'I'm afraid I need to.'

Suddenly she didn't want to discuss her private life
any more. She didn't want to let this nice, handsome
man know all about her past and the reasons for her
moving from the small hospital at Mayside to this
large, anonymous hospital where no one knew her
story. Where no one knew she was the surrogate
mother of a baby. Where no one could criticise her
like Annie had done, looking at her as if she were
unnatural in wanting to do what she'd done for her
sister. Most of all, she was in no mood for telling
anyone about the car accident that had changed her
life. How she was now a single mother bringing up
a baby, a baby who should have belonged to her
sister and brother-in-law.

There was a pause. Trudi and Dan looked at each
other. Reality hit them at the same time—there was

a line of sick children waiting to be examined and here they were, chatting idly about crèches!

Trudi gathered Grace to her and jumped up.

'Thanks again for putting my mind at rest. Maybe I'll see you in a couple of months' time when I start work again.' Her heart was pounding.

She found Dan breathtakingly attractive and could hardly believe that they were going to be working together in the very near future. She knew nothing about him, of course. He could turn out to be a rat like the majority of men she fancied. After all, she hadn't been given a very good 'husband and father' role model in her own father, who must have been one of the most recklessly irresponsible people of all time, if only half the stories she'd heard about him were true.

'Yes.' Dan rose from his chair. 'Goodbye, Mrs Younghouse...and Grace.'

He watched them both leave. She'd reminded him very much of a former girlfriend, that same upper-class accent, that same confidence that came from generations of breeding. But even in that brief consultation she'd come across as a much warmer, more genuine person than Jasmine had ever been. What a pity she was probably 'Mrs' Younghouse and not 'Miss' Younghouse. He found himself envying the fortunate Mr Younghouse, whoever he was.

'Lucky devil,' he muttered to himself.

CHAPTER TWO

'I'M taking five days off, starting the fifteenth,' stated Karen with determination.

'But I put my name down on the holiday list for those same days,' snapped Shelly. 'You know we can't both be away at the same time and I got my name down first!'

'That's just typical, isn't it?' retorted the red-faced Karen. 'She always jumps in just when she knows I'm going on holiday with Kev!'

'Excuse me,' replied Shelly calmly, pointing to the holiday rota pinned behind Trudi's desk, 'but I put my name down on that list and you didn't!'

'I told you I was going away with Kev to that motorbike rally on the Isle of Man and so what did you do? Sneaked in here and put your name down first!'

The two young nurses would have come to blows if Trudi hadn't jumped up from her desk and put her hands in the air.

'Now stop this, both of you! I don't know if you're trying this on me because I'm new to the job, but you'd better learn it won't work.' She turned to the rota chart. 'Shelly put her name down for those days and you, Karen, didn't.'

Karen was about to open her mouth but Trudi silenced her with a fierce look.

'In future, Karen, I suggest you put your name

down on the chart before revealing your holiday plans with Kev. OK? Now let's get back to work. We have patients to deal with.'

The two girls answered in unison. 'Yes, Trudi.'

Karen, crestfallen, sloped out of the office, followed by a triumphant Shelly.

Trudi rubbed her forehead and took a deep breath. This was the second day in her new job as the sister in charge of the Highfield outpatients department and she was sick of it already!

It wasn't so much the job itself, which she was sure she'd grow to like in time—it was the way she was expected to handle all the personality clashes that were emerging at a frightening rate. One person seemed to be a particular troublemaker—Shelly. Trudi recognised the type. Sexy, spoilt and spiteful. She would have to keep her eye on that madam or the morale of the whole department would suffer.

'I hate office politics!' Trudi clenched her fists in frustration. What she really wanted to do was to get back to 'proper' nursing—on a ward, with sick people who needed her. Or even to go medical school and train to be a doctor. Instead, she was landed with this outpatients job. And all because…

Damn. She mustn't think this way. She was grateful enough to be offered this position at Highfield—a rare nine-to-five job. It meant she could live some sort of normal life with Grace. The baby had settled in well at the hospital crèche and in later years when Grace was at school she would just need to cover the few out-of-school hours she would be working—and, of course, school holidays.

How her life had changed in just six months! Her

whole future was now totally different from what she'd imagined it was going to be.

Until the fatal car crash on the day Grace had been born, Trudi had planned to pick up her medical career the moment she felt recovered from the birth. When she'd been eight months pregnant she'd even applied for a place in medical school and had sent off the forms the week before the baby had been due.

She'd decided that after the baby was born and had been handed over to her sister, she would need a complete change of direction to take her mind off whatever emotional ties might have built up. *You'll never be able to give it up!* Annie's words had been a great worry to her and that had been why she'd needed to change her life—just in case her former best friend had proved right after all.

Fate had changed all that. She couldn't have foreseen the different kind of problems which had been lying ahead for her, the problems of looking after a baby and earning a living at the same time. She hadn't been left entirely destitute, having inherited some money from her sister, and this had been enough to pay for a small house. But she'd still needed to work to bring in an income for them both.

She'd moved away from her home town, fearing that more of her so-called friends would have Annie's 'shocked' attitude to her surrogate pregnancy if they found out, but that meant she was now totally on her own with no one to give her support, particularly emotional support. But she did have Grace, her darling baby...the only good thing to have come out of this whole mess. She hated herself for admitting it, but Annie had been right all along. She would have found it hard to give her daughter up. But she loved her sister so much that she wouldn't have been able to let her down either. Maybe one day she would get in touch with Annie and pick up the strands of their friendship. She missed her very much.

Shelly strode in through the open door and Trudi snapped back to the present.

'It's the cardiac clinic this morning and Dr Donovan's secretary hasn't sent down the files yet. Shall I phone her and tell her you're very cross about it?'

She's at it again, surmised Trudi. What a little troublemaker.

'I don't think that's a good idea, Shelly. I'll phone his secretary myself. Just give me the extension number.' Trudi was having to feel her way very gently in her new job and she wasn't being helped by this nurse who seemed to enjoy stirring it whenever possible.

'The extension numbers of the specialists are on the computer screen. Shall I work it for you and show you how to do it?' Smugness seemed to ooze out of Shelly's pores.

'If you would, please. And while you're at it, print me out the list as I'll find it more useful until I get familiar with the various systems.'

'Oh, here's a sheet printed out already.' Shelly opened a desk drawer and handed the page sweetly to Trudi.

'Thank you,' said Trudi dismissively through gritted teeth.

'Oh, and thanks about sorting out the holiday

problem,' said Shelly on the way out. 'I think you'll find Karen's a bit like that. You know, forgetful.'

What a minx! Trudi could see she was going to have to watch that young lady.

She'd no sooner dialled the secretary's extension when Shelly was back in the room, waving a set of files which she plonked on her desk.

'Karen had them all the time. See what I mean?' She gave a shrug and raised her eyes ceilingwards.

By now the phone had been answered. 'Dr Donovan's office,' said the clipped tones.

'I'm sorry about that,' said an embarrassed Trudi. 'I dialled you in error.'

Dan was on his way to his outpatients clinic when he noticed a vaguely familiar face in the corridor. It was that young woman whom he'd found so attractive in his first week when she'd brought her baby in with a suspected heart murmur. The one with the posh voice. She looked even prettier today, he noted, in her blue uniform.

'Hi,' he said. 'So we meet again.'

Trudi found herself looking up into the sexy brown eyes of the man who, two months ago, made such an impression on her. His looks, his voice, his manner—everything about him projected an animal magnetism that made her legs turn to water.

'Oh, hi. I mean, good morning, Dr Donovan.'

'Please, call me Dan. All the children on the wards do.'

'Hi, Dan—I'm Trudi.'

His smile bathed her in a warm glow so that she

quite forgot how stressed she'd been a moment ago. Shelly and her shenanigans seemed an ocean away.

The morning's list was going well, the system ticking along smoothly and incident-free. Shelly and Karen escorted the young patients, preparing them for Dan's examination, while Trudi assisted Dan, setting up ECGs and arranging with the radiographer for X-rays to be taken.

The children who entered the clinic with consternation written over most of their faces left with beams and cheery waves. Even the babies in the arms of anxious mothers and fathers left in happier moods than when they'd come in.

Except for one.

Jason Farquahar, a pasty-looking ten-year-old, was the last patient on the list and becoming bored sitting next to his mother, waiting to be called. Trudi thought Mrs Farquahar looked familiar and recalled that she'd seen her in one of the local village shops…a rather impatient, pushy woman.

'I've seen all those,' he said to her, indicating the pile of children's comics and books. His mother, who didn't appear to care one way or the other, hardly spoke a word to him. She kept giving big sighs and looking at her watch to check the time. What he really wanted, he told her, was a can of carbonated drink from the machine on the wall next to Trudi's desk. His mother gave him some money and the boy sauntered over to the machine.

Trudi caught his eye as he passed and smiled at him. His pale face had an elfin appeal about it and when he returned her smile he was transformed into a very captivating young man.

He's going to be a stunner when he's a few years older, predicted Trudi. A real heart-breaker.

As Jason opened the can's ring pull and took the first swig he walked over to Trudi.

'Nice place, this,' he said. 'Nice drinks, anyway.'

'Is this your first time here?' asked Trudi.

'Yeah. First time I've been in any hospital,' said Jason, adding, 'I've been in a vet's…which I suppose is a bit like it, really.'

'I suppose so,' said Trudi, not sure how to take Jason's remark.

'But, of course, in a vet's there's lots of animals waiting to be seen, not babies and children and all that.' Jason was becoming very animated and chatty. She would never have guessed he would have been like that from watching him sitting sullenly next to his mother.

'And a vet's is different because it's smaller than a hospital,' he continued between swigs of cola. 'Different smell as well.'

'I should hope so!' Trudi laughed, unable to help herself from giggling at the very idea of comparing her outpatients clinic with a vet's waiting room.

'My name's Jason. What's yours?'

'Trudi.'

'Will you come in with us to see the doctor?' asked Jason anxiously, his face now back to serious mode.

'Of course I'll come in if you want me to,' reassured Trudi. 'But you needn't be nervous about seeing the specialist. He's called Dan and he's not at all frightening.'

When the time came for Jason's case, Trudi took him and his mother into the room and introduced them to Dan who'd already familiarised himself with the details of the case.

'Your legs have been feeling numb, is that right, Jason? When did that start?'

'I think it was about a year ago, at first just a little bit. And then it started to get worse.'

'Did anything else happen. Headaches?'

'Yes. And I sometimes feel giddy.'

'What about school—can you play games? Football?'

'No. Not any more.' A sad expression came over Jason's pale face.

'Let's examine you, Jason, and see if we can't put that right. I always like to get my patients playing football if I possibly can and I'm sure you'll be no exception.'

Jason went enthusiastically to the examination table.

While this was going on, Trudi was talking quietly to Jason's mother who occasionally looked over in the direction of the examination table.

'How long will this take?' she asked Trudi. 'I can't spend all day here, you know. I've got a hair appointment soon. What's taking so long?'

'The specialist is just checking him over, listening to his chest, taking his pulse, that kind of thing. Your son is being given a thorough examination to try and find out why he's getting this numbness in his legs.'

Mrs Farquahar didn't seem particularly worried

about her son, noted Trudi. More irritated that she might miss her hair appointment! Perhaps it was just her way of showing concern, she surmised.

'Your GP might have thought there could be a cardiac problem.' She hesitated to use the word 'heart' in case it sent Mrs Farquahar into a panic, but she wanted the woman to know that her son's condition was worth spending some time over and, if necessary, worth missing a trip to the hair salon.

Over the other side of the room Dan had finished his preliminary examination of Jason who was now buttoning up his shirt. Dan walked over to where the boy's mother was sitting with Trudi.

'We need to do some more tests, Mrs Farquahar—just an ECG. To save you coming back another day, Sister Younghouse is going to fix it up now. I'd also like to have a chest X-ray of Jason and—'

Mrs Farquahar jumped up, gathering her handbag to her.

'We can't do it now. Come on, Jason, we're leaving.'

Dan moved in front of her, speaking in a quiet but firm voice.

'Mrs Farquahar, we suspect Jason may be suffering from a condition called coarctation, a narrowing of the aorta. If he is, we can probably put it right, so there's no need for you to worry at this stage. But we must find out what the situation is very soon.'

Dan steered her to a wall-chart of a cross-section of the heart, showing its structure and close-up enlargements of the valves.

'If Jason has what we suspect, there will be a narrowing in this area.' He pointed to the site of the ligament between the aorta and the pulmonary artery. 'It's a defect in the closing mechanism of the ductus arteriosus. It's a birth abnormality, more common in boys than girls. It often goes undiagnosed in infancy and symptoms only start occurring as the children get older.'

'I've never heard of that thing…what did you call it?'

'Coarctation.'

'I've never heard of this coarctation thing.'

She said the words almost dismissively, as if, because she hadn't heard of it, it couldn't exist. She glanced at her watch again and then, ignoring Dan, walked over to where Jason was sitting on the examination table, his thin legs swinging over the side.

'Put your jeans on, Jason, we must be going.'

'I strongly advise you to allow Jason to have the ECG and X-ray now, Mrs Farquahar. Jason could be very seriously ill,' Dan said, annoyed that he was being prevented from doing what he considered was in the best interests of his young patient.

But he may as well having been talking to himself. Within seconds, mother and child were gone, leaving a very angry Dan Donovan.

He flicked Jason's file shut.

'He must have an X-ray and ECG as soon as possible. If he's got what I think he has, that child could suffer heart failure at any time.'

By the end of her first week Trudi was beginning to get into the swing of things at the Highfield outpatients department.

She'd formed a good working relationship with

most of the staff and even Shelly appeared to have got the message that Trudi had the measure of her and her little tricks. She'd also made friends with most of the consultants whose clinics she ran and—most importantly—with their various secretaries.

Grace had settled in well at the crèche so that was one less worry, thought Trudi as she went to pick her up on the Friday evening.

She got chatting with another mother who had two children at the crèche, a toddler and a baby.

'How old are they?' asked Trudi, admiring the chubby, curly-haired boys in the double pushchair.

'Twenty months and nine months,' said the dark-haired young woman. 'I know!' she said, laughing at Trudi's sharp intake of breath. 'I've also got a three-year-old at nursery school and, believe me, this is the lot as far as I'm concerned. My husband went and had the snip last week!'

'The snip?'

'Vasectomy. He was as surprised as I was to have three babies in four years. But now we've got our three little boys we're delighted with them. But enough's enough, as they say.' The young woman smiled. 'My name's Clare. I saw you picking up your baby a couple of days ago. She's a real sweetie. What's her name?'

'Grace. And I'm Trudi. Nice to meet you, Clare.'

'Ah!' said Clare knowingly. 'I'll bet you're the Trudi my brother was talking about. Do you run the outpatients clinic?'

'Yes, I do.' Trudi was curious. 'So who is your brother?'

'Dan Donovan, the cardiologist.'

'He mentioned me?' She was even more curious now.

'He mentioned you twice, actually,' said Clare, amused.

'I find that very strange.' Strange, and also a little flattering, thought Trudi. Dan Donovan, in her estimation, was the most gorgeous man in the hospital—or anywhere else for that matter. Everything about him attracted her. Every time she spoke to him, on the phone or in person, or whenever she saw him in the clinic, she felt a disturbing thrill race through her.

'The first time he mentioned you was when you brought your baby in for a check-up.'

'Yes, that's right,' confirmed Trudi. Her mind flashed back to that consultation. She remembered how Dan had wanted to talk to her on a personal level, quizzing her about all sorts of things. At the time she hadn't been sure if that had been just his friendly manner or whether he'd truly been interested in her. It wasn't a subject she dwelt on too often…men who showed an interest in her. She was hardly in a position to start a relationship with Dan or anybody else now that she was a single mother—a single mother with a secret past that she was unwilling to divulge to anyone. Added to which, she was still very fragile emotionally, still coming to terms with her sister's sudden death.

'Dan was quite taken with you, I can tell you!' Clare laughed as they walked along to the car park, pushing their babies.

Trudi found herself blushing at this remark. Why on earth should Clare say such things? Was she also a troublemaker, like Shelly?

'Dan's a confirmed bachelor,' continued Clare, oblivious to Trudi's reaction. 'He's spent so much time and effort pushing his career along that he's had no time for marriage. "When the right girl comes along there'll be no holding me back!" is what he keeps on saying. But, honestly, Trudi, with the hours he works, plus the studying and lecturing and goodness know what else he does to further his career, he's never going to give himself the time or opportunity to meet the right girl, is he?'

Trudi nodded. 'Yes. I mean, no, he's not.'

'Ambition is all very well, but a bit of private life wouldn't do him any harm at all. Do him a lot of good, in fact. As a cardiologist he should know that. I keep telling him, "All work and no play is not good for your arteries." But he just changes the subject. He did have a serious girlfriend a few months ago, but that came to nothing, more's the pity.'

'So how did he come to mention me?' Trudi was wondering where this conversation was leading.

'A couple of months ago, Dan was at our house, visiting his nephews—whom he adores—when out of the blue he mentioned you! "Met this great-looking woman today and she's going to be working at Highfield," he said. And when I hugged him, thinking, wedding bells at last, he smiled that cheeky smile and said, "But she's already married, so that's my bad luck!" I could have brained him, getting me all excited over nothing. I was almost planning my wedding outfit and visualising the children as page-boys!'

Trudi was astonished. Imagine Dan bothering to mention her after that first meeting at the clinic! And telling his sister that she was 'great-looking'. But perhaps she shouldn't read too much into it. He was probably just saying that to keep his sister happy— to let her know that he hadn't stopped noticing women.

'Then earlier this week,' continued Clare, 'when he came over for a meal, he had a gleam in his eye and virtually the first thing he said was, ''You remember that great-looking woman I told you about, the married one? She's now working at the hospital in charge of Outpatients and her name's Trudi.'' I think he keeps mentioning you to keep me off the subject of marriage. I mean, he probably thinks that if he says the woman he fancies is married, that'll shut me up about weddings!'

Clare had reached her car and was digging in her shoulder-bag for the keys.

'So you think Dan was just mentioning me to get him off the hook, do you? To stop you nagging him to get married?' Trudi sounded a little disappointed. Although she knew nothing would have come of it, she'd still felt thrilled at the knowledge that Dan fancied her. Now, she realised, it had all been made up to keep his sister quiet.

'Looks like it, doesn't it? Oh, here they are!' said Clare, who'd eventually located her keys. 'Better not tell your husband! He might not find it so amusing!'

'Oh, I'm not married,' blurted Trudi before she could stop herself. She saw Clare look at her, then at baby Grace.

'I'm sorry, Trudi, I just presumed…you know…'

'I'm not married…any more.' added Trudi hastily.

This conversation was beginning to move into realms she was keen to avoid.

'Grace's father died before she was born,' she said, repeating the line she now gave to anyone who made enquiries of a similar nature.

'I am sorry, Trudi,' said Clare, putting a comforting hand on her arm. 'How terrible for you. Me and my big mouth! Look, just forget what I've said about Dan and everything. I feel awful about it.'

'No need to.' Trudi couldn't wait to get to her own car and extricate herself from this conversation. She was terrified that if Clare sympathised any further she might be tempted to blurt out the whole story and that would be fatal. Fatal to her new life and new job. She'd built a protective wall around herself and her baby and no one was going to knock it down.

'See you around, Clare.' Trudi moved off swiftly to her own car at the far end of the car park.

The weekend went far too quickly.

Trudi made sure that she spent every single moment with Grace to make up for the hours she'd had to leave her in the crèche. Grace didn't seem to have missed Trudi at all! But Trudi had certainly missed her. During her working days she constantly had the baby on her mind, wondering if Grace was crying or refusing her food or any of the hundreds of worries a mother had when she was parted from her baby for the first time. She was able to pop along to the crèche in her lunch-breaks and it was very reassuring to know Grace was on the premises and being looked after by qualified nursery nurses.

'She's a really happy, contented baby,' they'd told

Trudi. 'She's fast becoming one of our favourites because she never stops smiling.'

Trudi was grateful that Grace had settled in so well, but she was also experiencing mixed emotions about it. All those smiles were usually reserved for her and not the nursery nurses. It was hard to accept that she now had to share her little girl with others—babies grew up so quickly and she didn't want to miss a moment of it. But she knew she had to, like so many other working mothers. And she had to work full time, meaning she never really got to see Grace at her best during the week. By the time she got her home there was just time for her bath and feed and then bed.

Even though Trudi had to work full time, she realised she was lucky in other ways. She had her own home, bought with the money left to her by Jane and Rob. It wasn't much—they'd mortgaged their own home in order to finance years of fertility treatment. But the money they had left meant she was able to buy a cosy terraced cottage in a pretty village only a few miles away from the centre of the town where she now worked.

On Sunday, Trudi took Grace for some fresh air around the country lanes and through the fields where there were footpaths wide enough to take a pushchair. For safety she took along her neighbour's large dog, Bonzo.

She also had with her a small box with ventilation holes in the lid.

'We're going to collect ladybirds,' she told Grace as she slipped the box into the shopping basket that hung underneath the baby buggy. 'Then we'll bring

them back home and release them in our garden to
eat the greenfly.' Grace smiled back at Trudi.

'Sometimes I think you understand every word I
say, my little angel. Which is more than can be said
for you, you great brute. Stop pulling, Bonzo. I'll
only let you off the lead if you're going to behave
yourself.'

The three of them set off and were soon in open
country. Bonzo was let off the lead and bounded
ahead, but he always came back whenever Trudi
called him.

'You're not such a bad old thing after all,' she
said, patting him on the rump before throwing another stick for him to retrieve.

When they'd been going for about a mile, they
came upon a large house in extensive grounds sur-
rounded by a tall hedge. Peeping through the hedge,
which was wild and overgrown, Trudi could just
make out the house. It was very old and its air of
faded grandeur made it look as if it had seen better
days. It was the kind of house Trudi would have
loved to have lived in—after she'd spent a small for-
tune on renovation work. The garden wasn't at all
what she'd expected to see as she moved a few more
branches of the hedgerow to get a better view.

The lawns were very overgrown but in an attractive 'wildflower meadow' way. There were no
flower-beds, just rows and rows of fruit and vegetables.

'Ouch,' she said, catching her hand on a bramble.
'Serves me right for being a Nosy Parker. But look,
Grace, there are lots of ladybirds here.'

She bent down to pick up the box and was startled

by a man's voice behind her. She swung round, dropping the box, and came face-to-face with a tough-looking man with black hair.

'What are you doing?' he asked.

Trudi became very scared and, before answering, shouted, 'Bonzo!' The dog came hurtling back to Trudi's side and started to growl at the man.

'You've got a nerve, setting your dog on me on my own land! If you're going to play that game I have three Dobermans I can whistle for.'

The man had a very superior air which she found very threatening.

'Please, don't do that!' said Trudi in alarm. 'It's just that you gave me a fright, creeping up on me like that.'

'I wasn't creeping up on you. I live here. And I'd like to know what you're doing with my hedge, on my land. I saw you fiddling about with it. It's a very valuable hedge—valuable to wildlife—and I'd like to know what's in that box.'

His aggressive manner intimidated Trudi who began to stammer.

'I was j-just collecting ladyb-birds.'

'Why?'

'To put in my garden. There are lots of greenfly and I don't want to use chemicals on them…so I thought I'd get some ladyb-birds.' She realised how foolish she must have sounded, but, instead of laughing or shouting at her again, the man's whole attitude changed in an instant.

'Quite right, quite right. All these chemicals are ruining the planet. We're poisoning the land…

there'll be nothing left except barren earth. We're destroying Mother Nature, don't you agree?'

His change of mood took her by surprise.

'I suppose so.' Trudi nodded, picking up her box and surreptitiously trying to move away.

'Please, stay,' he said, now smiling broadly at her, his hair flying wildly in the wind. 'You're welcome to collect ladybirds. Help yourself.'

He turned to walk away. Trudi had to grab Bonzo's collar to stop him chasing after the man and giving him a nip on the leg. Whether or not this strange man owned the large house and land, she wasn't staying around to find out. She just knew she was going to get out of there as soon as possible.

A small voice called through the hedge.

'Dad, who's that you're talking to?'

'Just somebody looking for ladybirds, that's all, Jason.'

'Oh,' said Trudi, realising for the first time to whom she'd been speaking. 'Are you the father of Jason Farquahar?'

'Yes. And who are you?'

'Trudi Younghouse. I work at Highfield Children's Hospital. I met Jason and your wife at the cardiac clinic on Tuesday.'

'Is that you, Trudi?' asked Jason through the hedge.

'Yes. How are you, Jason? How are the legs?' She tried to keep the enquiry light even though she knew the boy's medical situation could be very serious.

'Fine. Just a bit numb. Dad says it's nothing to worry about.'

'Nothing to worry about,' repeated his father.

Thinking on her feet, Trudi said quickly, 'Will you be bringing Jason in for those tests we told your wife about at the clinic, Mr Farquahar?'

'He's fine.'

'But he may not be,' persisted Trudi. 'Please, let him come in for the tests.'

'Just collect your ladybirds and then get off my land. OK?'

With an aggressive look on his face, Jason's father strode along and disappeared through a gap, previously unnoticed by Trudi, in the giant hedge.

Trudi left the Farquahars' land as quickly as she could, racing along with the pushchair and keeping Bonzo on the lead in case she had any other encounters of a similarly disturbing nature.

When they reached a main road she slowed down and caught her breath.

She couldn't get the Farquahars out of her mind. Both parents seemed oblivious to the fact that their son's life could be in danger. The mother appeared to be so wrapped up in her own life she couldn't even be bothered to cancel a hair appointment—and the father seemed equally oblivious to the possible dangers faced by his young son. The word 'neglect' sprang to mind. It wasn't the usual scenario, that was for sure—a boy from that background—but neglect wasn't confined to the underprivileged in society. It could just as easily be found among the gentry. As she herself knew only too well.

Dan's words came back to her. 'That child could suffer heart failure at any time.'

But what could she, or Dan for that matter, do about it?

Trudi was walking along, her mind occupied with these thoughts, not really concentrating on where she was headed. Grace started to whine a little bit. Trudi looked at her watch. With a shock she realised they'd been out for two hours and that Grace must be getting hungry by now. Where on earth were they?

Because she'd rushed off after her strange encounter with Mr Farquahar, she hadn't paid much attention to which direction she'd been going. The village she was approaching wasn't her own. She headed for a bus shelter which she spotted near the post office and general stores.

'We'll just have to get the bus home, won't we, Grace?'

Before she could reach it someone came out of the shop and called to her.

It was Dan! He smiled as he came running towards her, his dark hair ruffled, his body long and graceful in chinos and sweatshirt.

Her heart skipped a beat. Each time she saw him she was reminded just how disturbingly attractive he was—and his casual clothes just seemed to underline his striking good looks. She felt a prickle of sexual excitement as he spoke to her.

'Hello, Trudi. And baby Grace. And who's this great monster?' he asked, walking up to Bonzo who was eyeing him with suspicion. The dog growled and showed a mouthful of sharp teeth.

'Hey, you've got some guard dog there! What's his name?'

'Bonzo.'

Dan threw his head back and gave a loud guffaw.

'I don't believe it! You've got a dog called Bonzo!

Nobody really and truly has a dog called that, do they?'

Trudi laughed. 'He's my neighbour's dog and, yes, he really is called Bonzo. Though it gets embarrassing to have to shout his name out if anyone's listening! But he's a very good protector—just look how he's eyeing you up. He's fine when he sees that I'm friendly towards someone—otherwise he'll have your guts for garters.'

'Charming!'

'So what are you doing here?' Trudi asked.

'I was going to ask you the same question,' said Dan, walking along with her. 'I've been visiting my sister who lives in the village. How about you?'

'I live in the next village,' Trudi answered. 'At least I think I do. To tell the truth, I've become a bit disorientated and I'm not really sure where I am. I thought I'd get the bus back home or else I could be walking for hours.'

'You've missed the bus, I'm afraid,' said Dan.

'Oh, no. When?'

'Friday.'

Trudi's jaw dropped. 'I might have guessed there'd be no buses on Sunday.'

'No buses on Saturday either,' said Dan. 'There's one each weekday. And when I say one, I mean one. At nine o'clock in the morning and one back at five in the evening.'

Trudi looked crestfallen.

'Anyway, what kind of a knight in shining armour do you take me for?' teased Dan.

'I'm sorry?'

'Do you really think I'd let you struggle home on a bus with a small baby and a big dog when I have my car across the street?'

CHAPTER THREE

TRUDI accepted Dan's offer of a lift with gratitude and relief.

'I don't know what I'd have done if I hadn't bumped into you,' she said, lifting Grace and the ladybird box out of the buggy and following Bonzo into the back seat of Dan's car.

Dan folded the pushchair and loaded it into the boot.

'I'm sure you'd have found some way of coping,' he said gallantly. 'You could have phoned for a taxi from the shop.'

'I suppose so,' conceded Trudi. 'I just wasn't thinking straight after a peculiar encounter back there. You weren't the only person I bumped into today. I had a close encounter with Mr Farquahar—Jason's father. You remember, the child who urgently needs an ECG and X-ray?'

As they drove, Trudi told Dan all about it.

Dan had also been talking about Jason Farquahar to his sister.

'Clare was telling me about the family. She knows of them because her three-year-old goes to nursery school at the local village school which Jason attends. Some of her neighbours' children are in the same class as Jason and they all say what a nice kid he is. But his parents are considered to be totally useless. Lots of money but no sense. And not much

42

time for Jason, from all accounts. Neither of them ever turns up on parents' day, and they never come to any of the school concerts.'

'What a shame. Poor Jason. Does Clare know him?'

'By sight. And she mentioned how pale he's been looking recently. She said he looked as if he was at death's door—and after examining him at the clinic last week I think she could be right. If he's got co-arctation he's lucky to have reached the age of ten without major heart problems. If anything goes wrong his parents will have a lot to answer for.'

'It's terrible,' said Trudi. 'I feel we're so helpless in Jason's case. You don't think of those kind of people being a problem. A deprived childhood usually involves grinding poverty. You don't expect to find social workers beating a path to the door of Jason's kind of family. And yet I think Jason is a neglected child.' She spoke with feeling. She and Jane had most definitely been neglected by their parents, aristocratic titles notwithstanding.

'Couldn't agree more,' said Dan. 'But let's talk about more cheerful things. Apart from that, did you enjoy your walk?'

'It was great. I love the country—such a nice change from working in town all week. How about you?'

'I've a flat in town. But, like you, I love the country and the open-air life. Even when I lived in London I would try and get away whenever I could—walking, sailing, that kind of thing.'

'Sailing?'

'I've a small boat which I sail from time to time.

In fact, I've just joined a sailing club near here—at Windmill Mere. My brother-in-law promises to come and crew for me.'

'The one who's had a vasectomy?' asked Trudi, recalling her conversation in the car park with Clare. 'Oh, turn left here. My house is on the right, next to the end terrace.'

Dan swerved as he turned, almost mounting the pavement.

'I'm sorry,' apologised Trudi. 'I didn't give you much notice of that turning.'

'It wasn't that.' Dan laughed. 'It was the vasectomy bit that startled me! You're full of surprises, Trudi! How on earth did you know Jim has had a vasectomy?'

'Clare told me when we met at the crèche. We didn't just talk about that, of course!'

We talked about you fancying me, mused Trudi, but then it turned out to be nothing of the kind.

By now Dan had pulled up outside her house. 'This one?'

'Yes.'

Dan took the pushchair out of the boot and opened the back doors of the car, which had childproof locks, to let Trudi, Grace and Bonzo out. The dog went rushing out and up the path of the house next door, disappearing round the side of the terrace, trailing his lead behind him.

'Where on earth's he gone?' said Dan in annoyance.

'Home. He lives next door to me. I think he's getting rather hungry. And the same goes for this little one.'

Trudi put Grace in her buggy and pushed her towards the house. Sliding her key into the lock, she pushed open the front door.

'Thanks, Dan,' she said, pulling the buggy over the doorstep. 'I really do appreciate the lift. I'd ask you in for a coffee but I must feed Grace.'

But Dan didn't appear to have heard her. Or, if he had, he'd chosen to ignore it. He shut and locked the car doors and followed her to the house and over the threshold.

'Yes, a coffee would be great,' he said, holding the pushchair while she picked up Grace. 'I'll make us some while you see to madam.'

It was strange, having a man in the house. As Trudi fed Grace in the small kitchen, Dan busied himself making two mugs of instant coffee. He placed Trudi's on the table and then sat opposite her, drinking contentedly from his mug of coffee. He didn't take his eyes off her, Trudi noticed. At least, whenever she glanced up, Dan's eyes met hers. It was becoming a little embarrassing.

'Am I making you feel uncomfortable?' he asked, noticing the way she kept avoiding his gaze.

'No,' she lied. 'I'm just not used to have a man— or anyone, really—in the house.'

Then it was Dan's turn to feel embarrassment. 'I'm sorry, Trudi. How thoughtless of me. I'd forgotten for a moment about your husband. Clare told me about it and how he died before Grace was born. I'll go, shall I? It was very heavy-handed of me to push my way in when you're still getting over his death.'

His words made Trudi's hand shake so much that the feeding bottle nearly slipped out of her hold.

'You don't need to go, Dan. Not for that reason, anyway. I'm fine, really, I'm fine.' Please, let him change the subject, prayed Trudi.

'Was your husband in medicine?' he continued.

'No.'

Trudi shifted nervously in her seat. Dan began to get the message that his line of questioning was intrusive.

'I just thought it might help to talk about it, that's all. It's all part of the grieving process.'

'Not for me,' said Trudi firmly. 'I don't want to talk about it, with you or anyone else. OK?'

Dan put his mug down on the scrubbed pine table.

'I was only talking about it because...' He couldn't finish the sentence as he hadn't put his thoughts together on the subject. Why was he so interested in her present situation? Was it because he knew she was no longer married and was, therefore, possibly available?

Putting it that way, it made him and his questioning seem crude and callous...and calculating. But it wasn't like that. *He* wasn't like that. What Dan felt for Trudi was something he was unable to put into words. It was a feeling, an emotion he'd never experienced before. A longing to protect her, to look after her. She was so vulnerable...a woman alone. A very attractive woman alone.

He stood up to leave, feeling he'd outstayed his welcome.

'Please don't feel you have to leave, Dan.'

'Yes, I do,' he replied. 'I've got an appointment...with the laundrette.'

Trudi laughed. It was a lovely sound and made his

heart leap. The more he saw of her the more he realised how unlike Jasmine she was. Jasmine had the same tall, slim, sexy figure as Trudi, a figure that promised hot nights… But there was a touch of calculating self-interest and phoniness about his former girlfriend. Trudi, unless he was very much mistaken, was genuine through and through.

'I'll let myself out. See you at the hospital.'

He walked to the door and turned to look at her once more before finally taking his leave. Her tousled auburn hair was falling over her face as she cradled the baby nestling in the crook of her arm, tilting the bottle for the last few drops of the feed. It was an image he couldn't get out of his mind as he drove back into town.

Don't rush her, he warned himself. Take your time, Dan.

He knew he wouldn't, of course. Like most medics, Dan was absolutely hopeless at listening to his own advice.

Monday morning and back to the grindstone. Trudi imagined that starting her second week would be a good deal easier than the first. But it wasn't.

It was just as bad and possibly even a little worse. More things seemed to go wrong, more patients' files were lost or misplaced and the staff, particularly Shelly, were making her day more problematic than necessary.

'Someone in your department has just been extremely rude to me,' said the irate voice at the other end of the phone. Mrs Duncan wasn't in the best of moods and it became apparent during the conversation that Shelly was to blame for offending the general surgeon's secretary.

Monday was the day for the general surgery clinic, which was taken by Mr Davis, the paediatric general surgeon, or his senior registrar, Dr Phil Porter. It was too much to hope it was going to run smoothly, thought Trudi with a sigh, now that Shelly had ruffled the feathers of the very influential Mrs Duncan.

Trudi did her best to calm her down, without appearing to be critical of one of her staff.

'Shelly,' she told the sulky nurse afterwards, 'I think it's best if I speak to Mrs Duncan in future. If there's anything that needs sorting out just come to me first.'

'I suppose the snooty old cow's been on to you, complaining about me, has she?' Shelly was quite unrepentant and Trudi didn't have the stomach for a full-scale showdown so she let it go. There was a line of patients waiting for the clinic to start and Dr Porter had just buzzed to indicate that he was ready for the first one.

At eleven-thirty, as she was snatching a quick coffee-break, Trudi was surprised by a visit from Dan.

'The cardiac clinic's tomorrow, isn't it?' she asked, wondering if the day had been changed without her knowledge. Something else Shelly had kept from her, perhaps?

'Nothing to do with the clinic,' said Dan. 'Although I suppose in a way it is. I've just had a phone call from Jason Farquahar's GP. He wanted to know the outcome of my examination last week. He wasn't too pleased when I told him we were unable to carry out some vital tests to establish whether Jason does have a problem with his aorta.'

Trudi was defensive. 'But the mother took the child away before we could do the tests!'

'That's what I told him. He then said that the headmistress of the village school had phoned him this morning to say that she'd to send Jason home because she was so concerned about his health. The child could barely walk, she said.'

'What on earth can we do about it? Maybe you should get the GP to phone the police or Social Services?'

Dan paused for a moment. 'I don't think we've reached that stage yet. In any event, the GP is in a difficult situation because he referred the case to us. As far as he was concerned, we had it in hand. I told him that I'd written to him, explaining the situation, but the letter must have gone astray.'

'So where's Jason now?' Trudi recalled the pale, elfin-faced boy who had chatted so amiably to her the previous week, and whose plaintive voice she'd heard through the hedge, assuring her of his faith in his dad's judgement that there was nothing to worry about.

'The headmistress said Jason's mother came, grudgingly, and collected him. But she felt so concerned she rang his doctor.' Dan was crestfallen. 'I feel we've let the lad down. Badly.'

'What else could we have done?' Trudi also felt a responsibility for Jason even though she was at a loss to know what to do next.

'I'm planning on going over to the Farquahars' place and having a word with the parents. Perhaps if

I stress the urgency of the matter they'll let me take their son to hospital for the tests.' Dan checked his watch. 'I thought I'd go at lunchtime. I wondered if you wanted to come along. I would certainly appreciate a bit of back-up.'

'Sure,' said Trudi, glad to be asked. 'I've been feeling guilty about Jason, too.'

'Pick you up outside the clinic entrance just before one o'clock.'

As she slipped into the passenger seat of Dan's car she asked, 'Should I put a coat over this, do you think?'

Dan cast an appreciative eye over the slim figure in the dark blue uniform.

'No,' he said decisively. 'It makes our surprise visit to the Farquahars look more official. Gives it that "medical" look. Dressed in a suit, I could be anyone—but you really look the part.'

As they sped away, Trudi realised this was the first time she and Dan had been alone together. At all their previous meetings there had always been someone else present, even if it had only been baby Grace.

She cast a surreptitious glance at him. His face in profile could only be described in one word…handsome. A good-shaped nose, not too big, not too small. High cheek-bones and a strong chin. His hair, so dark it was almost black, was attractively close-cropped, short but not too short.

Men hadn't figured much in Trudi's life in the past couple of years. She'd almost forgotten what it was like to be alone with one…with one she found desperately attractive, that was. There hadn't been that many men in her life. Twice she'd thought she'd been in love—but she hadn't been. When the relationships had ended, although she'd been hurt for a time she'd realised that they would never have worked in the long term…she wanted something better than those two particular men had been able to give her.

Before she'd embarked on the pregnancy for her sister, she'd just come out of the last relationship. Simon had been someone her sister and brother-in-law had strongly disapproved of. They hadn't been able to understand what Trudi had seen in him. Looking back on it now, neither could she.

Simon was a loner. Maybe that's what had attracted her to him in the first place. He'd played on Trudi's kind nature, making her feel that she'd had no choice but to stick by him and support him emotionally through all his ups and downs. It hadn't only been emotional support—she'd handed over increasingly large sums of money to him which he'd convinced her had been 'only loans'. She'd begun to suspect he'd had a drink problem and had persuaded him to get help. She'd been amazed how quickly he'd agreed to do so, and when he'd told her he was booking himself into a clinic she'd been, once again, very supportive. He just needed a bit of help with the fees, he'd said very plausibly. A thousand pounds had been what he'd asked her for. All Trudi had been able to offer him had been five hundred—all the savings she'd had. He'd taken it…and had disappeared.

'You gave him *five hundred quid*?' gasped her sister in disbelief. 'I always thought he was a con man and now he's proved it!'

Trudi was shattered. She had no idea that a man she'd once loved could have used her in such a way. How could she have been such a fool as to fall for the oldest trick in the book?

'What are you thinking about?' asked Dan. 'You're very quiet. Are you wondering what we're going to say to the Farquahars?'

Trudi clicked back to the present. 'What are we going to say?'

'I'll think of something,' Dan reassured her.

There was something very confident about Dan— and the nice thing was, his confidence rubbed off on those around him. Not only did Trudi like his looks, she liked his character as well. In fact, she couldn't think of a single thing about him that she didn't like! That was her problem—because she was sure that if he knew she'd misled him about the baby and her non-existent late husband, he might not be so keen to be her friend.

There would be some people, she realised, who would take the same stance as Annie over her surrogacy. Dan may also think it was a very odd thing to do as well. 'Unnatural' was how Annie had described it. Well, there was no turning back. She and Grace would face the world alone. They didn't need anyone…not if it meant being held up to ridicule or criticism. One thing was for sure, she wasn't going to tell Dan. She valued his friendship too much to put it at risk.

They drove up the lane leading to the Farquahars' mansion.

It was a different side of the house from where

Trudi had met the owner yesterday. This time they came upon large gates overgrown with brambles.

Dan got out and was about to open them when Trudi remembered something.

'Don't, Dan! He's got Dobermans. They might be roaming the grounds.'

Dan peered through the gates. 'Can't see any dogs. The gates aren't locked so I'll just open them quickly and we can drive up to the front door. If the dogs come out we can beat a hasty retreat.'

They both stood outside the imposing front door, having rung the doorbell several times. Dan was just about to start knocking with his fist when they heard the sound of dogs barking from the other side of the door.

'At least we know where the Dobermans are,' he said, taking a step backwards. 'Stand behind me, Trudi, in case the brutes come leaping out.'

'You're joking! I think we should both run back to the car.'

While they were debating the best course of action, they heard a man's voice calming the dogs and then a bolt rattled and the door opened to reveal a cross-looking Mr Farquahar.

He eyed them with suspicion as he held onto the collars of two large slavering dogs.

'Yes? What do you want?'

Trudi butted in first. 'Mr Farquahar, we met yesterday. Do you remember? I was the person collecting the ladybirds...for my garden.'

'Yes, I remember.' He turned to Dan. 'And who are you?'

'Dan Donovan.' He put out his hand but immediately withdrew it on seeing the vicious look in the Dobermans' eyes.

'Have you come for the organic vegetables we advertised? We've got a new crop of carrots freshly dug. I believe there are cabbages and beans as well.'

Trudi nodded enthusiastically before Dan could reply. 'We'd love some.' Under her breath she hissed to Dan, 'Let's just get inside the house!'

They followed Mr Farquahar into the oak-panelled hall.

As they passed through the large kitchen Trudi caught a glimpse of Mrs Farquahar disappearing into another room. Trudi went after her.

'Mrs Farquahar…Mrs Farquahar.'

Dan was close on her heels. They both followed the woman into the living room where, lying limply on a couch, was Jason. His mother turned to see who was following and calling after her. On seeing Trudi in her nurse's uniform, she recognised who she was. She scrutinised Dan and recognised him as well.

'What are you two doing here?' she asked aggressively.

Her husband had followed them into the room.

'They've come for a box of vegetables. I'm just about to sort it out for them.'

'But she's the nurse from the hospital, and he's the doctor!' The woman pointed a well-manicured finger in their direction.

'So do you want the vegetables or don't you?' He looked bored.

'Yes, please,' Trudi said hastily.

'We've also come to have a look at Jason,' answered Dan calmly. 'We had a phone call from your own doctor after the school had rung him. Jason could be much sicker than you think. Would you let me examine him, please?'

'You can if you like,' said his mother, unscrewing the lid from a bottle of nail varnish. 'Everyone's making a huge fuss over nothing. Jason's always had a pale colour. He'll be fine, eating the organic vegetables. Anyway, you'd better make your examination quick—not a long one like last time at the hospital. I nearly missed my hair appointment. And tonight I've got a dinner party to organise, so hurry up.'

'Jason needs more than organic vegetables, I would say. Just look at him, he's semi-conscious.' Dan moved towards the couch.

'Hello, Jason,' he said gently. 'How are you feeling?'

'Fine,' answered a small, weak voice.

'See, we told you there was nothing the matter with him,' said Mr Farquahar belligerently.

Dan knelt by the side of the couch and gave Jason a quick examination. When he'd listened to Jason's heartbeat and felt his pulse he became extremely concerned. Dan stood up and stepped towards the others, indicating that they should move a little distance away from Jason so the boy couldn't overhear too much of what he was going to say.

'Your son could be dying,' he said gravely, keeping his voice low. 'I want to take him back to the hospital with us right now. There could be no time to lose…if you want to save your son, that is.'

Even on hearing the seriousness of Dan's pronouncement, Mrs Farquahar reacted as if she hadn't taken it in and kept on painting her nails. Her husband, on the other hand, did appear to be concerned—and not a little guilty.

'Well, you'd better take him and make him better. I'll come along with you.'

Mrs Farquahar looked up reluctantly from her nail varnishing. 'Be back in time for the dinner party, won't you?'

Without responding to the woman—he didn't trust himself not to give her a good shaking—Dan went up to Jason and gathered him up in his arms.

Trudi went on ahead and opened the front door for them. Jason's father followed. He appeared struck dumb, the gravity of the situation only now hitting home.

CHAPTER FOUR

TRUDI manoeuvred the trolley up one of the dozens of aisles of the large supermarket on the outskirts of town.

Grace was propped up in the special baby seat and even at eight months was taking an interest in what was going on, her bright eyes following her mother's every move as she filled the trolley with mounds of groceries and baby goods.

'Disposable nappies, talcum powder, cotton wool, baby wipes.' Trudi reeled off the various items as she ticked them on her list.

'Who would have thought that one baby could account for such a mountain of stuff?' she said to Grace, who always enjoyed their trips to the supermarket. The bright colours of the packaging and the many aisle banners and hanging mobiles all served to make her feel that this was a really exciting place to be!

'Well, hello, there!' said a familiar voice. Trudi looked up from her shopping list and saw Dan coming towards her, pushing a smaller trolley.

It had been two months since the drama with the Farquahars. They'd got Jason to hospital in time for him to be operated on by the cadiothoracic surgeon, who'd repaired the heart defect. In a very short time Jason had been back home and was now—according to Clare—a healthy ten-year-old, running around the playground with all his school mates.

Trudi saw Dan each week at the cardiac clinic but hadn't had a chance to be alone with him very much in that time. He'd made sure she'd been kept up to date with Jason's progress, taking her into the ward after his operation and including her in his discussions with the surgeon. Apart from that, she'd rarely seen him.

Yet Trudi couldn't help thinking about him. Constantly. Thinking about him and fantasising. Imagining what it would be like to be married to him, or even just to be his girlfriend...his lover. Never before had she been so attracted to a man. His touch, no matter how fleeting, sent thrilling waves through her. Whenever she saw him her spirits leapt, and just a smile from him was guaranteed to make her day.

So it was again. Bumping into him at the supermarket, it had turned an ordinary shopping trip into the high spot of her day.

'Hello, Dan,' she responded. 'So even top consultants have to do their own shopping!'

'All my servants were busy.' His eyes were laughing as he held her gaze for an instant.

Trudi was fascinated by him. Increasingly, he was having this effect on her. When he looked at her he made her feel she was the only woman in the world. Did he have this effect on everyone? she wondered.

'You look as if you're preparing for a siege,' he said, taking in the mountain of shopping in her trolley. 'How long will that last?'

'Oh...two weeks, probably less!' said Trudi. 'Everything connected with a baby comes in such bulky packets.'

'That's something I've no experience of,' said Dan. 'I just see them stripped for an examination…as I did this little lady. No more worries about a heart murmur?'

'No, thank goodness. I think it was just an over-enthusiastic young doctor at the clinic. But he certainly gave me a nasty turn.'

'I'll keep my eye on her, if you like. I can call in and give her a quick check-up from time to time. Would that reassure you?'

'Thanks, Dan. Yes, it would.'

'Well, I mustn't delay you. You don't want to waste precious time talking to me when you could be enjoying yourself shopping!' He grinned at her, and looked very boyish, squeezing her arm as he went past.

Trudi's heart gave a lurch. His touch felt danger-ously sexy and, giving an involuntary shiver, she bur-ied her face in her shopping list.

'Paper tissues,' she muttered to herself as she pushed the trolley into the next aisle. Ten minutes later she'd almost finished her shopping.

'Just need bread,' she said to Grace as they headed for the in-store bakery. As she stood, selecting what she needed from the shelves, another familiar voice spoke to her.

'I don't believe this! It's you, isn't it, Trudi?' said a masculine voice with a distinctive cut-glass accent.

She swung round to find herself facing a most un-welcome reminder of the past. Simon.

Her ex-boyfriend had disappeared out of her life—

and with her money—almost two years previously. She was astonished to see him again. He looked very much as he had when she'd known him, smartly dressed in a well-tailored shirt and trousers and a genuine Barbour jacket. No cheap imitations for Simon for whom only the best would do. As long as someone else was paying.

'Simon!' she gasped. 'What are you doing here?'

'I live nearby,' he replied casually. 'Been here about a month, actually. So, what about you? Do you live near here?'

Alarm bells rang in her head. Don't tell him where you live or he'll be round cadging money or a bed—or both.

'I live in another village,' she answered vaguely. 'This is a good place to shop, that's all.' She could see Simon looking towards her trolley where Grace was gurgling in the baby seat.

'This yours?' he asked incredulously.

'She's my baby, yes.' That should put him off if anything would, surmised Trudi.

But Grace's presence only made Simon keener to talk.

'Fancy you being married. And with a baby!' He picked up Trudi's left hand and scrutinised it. Noting she wasn't wearing a ring, he looked quizzically at her. 'Single mum, eh?'

'That's right, Simon.'

'Very fashionable, so I hear.'

She could have brained him.

'I haven't become a single mother to be fashionable! What kind of woman do you take me for?'

He sidled up to her, slipping an arm around her

waist. 'Surely the Honourable Trudi Younghouse didn't find herself "in trouble",' he said huskily in a voice that he, mistakenly, believed was sexy. 'I thought it was only the lower orders who found themselves in that position. And, anyway, what do you think abortion's for?'

She pushed his arm away. 'I know what you're up to. You're trying to get me angry and upset, just like you always used to do. And then you'll apologise, like you always did, and expect me to forgive you. Well, Simon, I've learned my lesson the hard way with you, and you no longer have any hold over me. I got over you a long time ago.'

He took on a familiar look of hurt pride. 'Trudi, you misjudge me. You always did. I was only wanting to know how you were managing on your own with a baby. I'm sure you find it hard, don't you?'

She recognised his fishing technique. He was desperately trying to work out the situation and see if there was any way he could use it to his own advantage. He didn't care about her—he never had.

'Does the child's father give you any support?' he ventured. 'Have you found a rich sugar daddy?'

She could tell that Simon was sizing her up to see if there might be some more money forthcoming from her. Trudi nipped it in the bud.

'There's no sugar daddy. And, yes, it is hard, managing on my own, very hard. Especially as most of my spare money was given to some scoundrel who ran off with it.' She gave him a hard look.

'I hope that's not me you talking about, sweetheart. One of the reasons I came back was to find you and repay the loan.' He smiled at her in that familiar, plausible way he had. But this time she was ready for him.

'So you've come to repay the loan, have you?'

'Honestly. I even tried your old address and they said you'd left. Said you'd left Mayside Hospital, too.'

'You went to my old address? And to the hospital?' Trudi was taken aback.

'They said you'd moved away,' Simon continued. 'Isn't it amazing we should bump into each other here? So, where do you work now?'

Before she could check herself she'd blurted out, 'Highfield Children's Hospital.' Annoyed that she'd let him get more information out of her than she'd intended giving, she went on the attack.

'So, where have you been all these years? Why did you just disappear without saying a word? Never mind the money, Simon, I thought we had a relationship. You could at least have said goodbye!'

He looked repentant. But, then, he always was a good actor, she reflected.

'I couldn't, Trudi. I had to get my head together and sort myself out at the clinic.'

'That was two years ago!'

'It took me a long time, believe me. I had years of alcoholism to fight. I didn't want to come back into your life until I'd conquered my addiction. You'd have given me a good tongue-lashing and quite right.'

My God, thought Trudi, he's even more plausible than before. Does he really believe I'm going to fall for that story? The truth is more likely to be that he's run out of funds and wants to sponge off me again.

'You've come back to repay the loan, you said?' This I've got to see, she reflected scornfully.

'Indeed. Just give me your address and I'll post it to you.'

'You can send it to me at the hospital,' she said firmly. 'Now we must get on.'

She dropped the bread in the trolley and pushed it towards the checkout. Simon followed.

'Here, let me help you with all that.'

Before she could stop him he was loading all her shopping onto the conveyor belt.

'I can manage, Simon.'

'Let me help. For old times' sake.' He slipped an arm round her shoulder and kissed her on the cheek. 'You still love me, don't you?' he whispered smoothly in her ear.

At that moment she looked across to the next checkout and found Dan's eyes boring into her. He was taking in everything. As his eyes met hers, he hastily looked down, picked up his groceries and walked out of the supermarket without a backward glance.

He didn't see Trudi push Simon away or hear her say to him, 'No, I don't love you. Now leave me alone or I'll scream!'

All Dan had seen was a well-heeled young man putting his arm around Trudi and kissing her. It had come as quite a shock to him, believing as he did that she was a woman alone, without close men friends or relatives. That was what she'd implied whenever he'd broached the subject. A widow she'd said she was. At least he thought she'd said as much. Maybe after all there *was* a man in her life. What an idiot he'd been! No wonder she hadn't wanted to ask him in for a coffee two months ago. She'd probably been expecting the boyfriend to turn up at any moment.

'It's really great, having a boyfriend with a motorbike,' bragged Karen, who'd been regaling the staff of the outpatients department with the details of her recent holiday with Kev.

Part of the pleasure for Karen in recounting her holiday adventures lay in the knowledge that Shelly was boyfriend-less at the present moment. Shelly may have won the battle for the chosen holiday dates, but Karen had Kev and, therefore, was one up on her colleague.

Shelly was fuming. 'I wouldn't look at anyone who just had a motorbike,' she snorted with contempt. 'You won't catch me hanging onto the back of some leather-clad nerd in a crash helmet. If a man can't afford a car he's of no interest to me.'

'You're just jealous,' sneered Karen.

'Jealous! Of you and Kev!'

'Yes. Because you haven't got a man—with a car *or* a motorbike!' As Karen spoke the words she caught Trudi's eye and her hand flew to her mouth, hoping that the staff sister didn't think she was commenting on her own particular man-free lifestyle.

'I'm just popping into the canteen for a quick lunch,' said Trudi, pretending she hadn't heard Karen's last remark. She'd taken all she could of the bickering between Karen and Shelly that particular Monday morning. A restful few minutes in the staff restaurant would help her relax before the afternoon clinic.

She was deep in thought when Dan walked up to her table and put his tray down.

'You were miles away!' He laughed. 'May I join you?'

'Please, do,' she said hastily, making room for him on the small table. A familiar sensual tingle rippled through her as it always did whenever she found herself in his presence.

'Can I get you a refill?' he asked, pointing to her empty coffee-cup.

'Yes, please, Dan.' She was glad he'd asked. It meant he wanted her to stay a little longer while he had his lunch, and Trudi had something she wanted to talk to him about.

When he'd settled down at the table and had begun unwrapping his sandwich from its Cellophane packet, she wasted no time.

'You know the other day, when we met at the supermarket?'

Dan looked up and nodded. How could he forget?

'That man you saw me with. He was a former boyfriend. Someone in my past.'

'I see.' Dan tried to keep his face unreadable, but he felt a sinking feeling in the pit of his stomach.

'I thought I should explain because it might have seemed as if he was still in my life.' Trudi was finding this harder than she'd expected. The more she explained about Simon the sillier she felt. Was she making a fool of herself by telling all this to Dan?

'I did wonder,' he said. A glimmer of hope had appeared.

Was it her imagination or did he look relieved?

'He came completely out of the blue,' she continued. Why did she feel the need to explain even further? Was it because of the look in Dan's eyes when he'd seen Simon kissing her?

'I see,' he repeated.

'And, like I said, Simon was from my past and, as far as I'm concerned, he can stay there.'

'Simon?'

'That's his name. My ex-boyfriend.'

'Ex-boyfriend,' stated Dan, placing emphasis on the 'ex'.

'Yes. He's a complete con man. He thought he was onto a good thing with me, thought he'd struck a rich vein.' She didn't want to go any further into the explanation, didn't want to mention anything else about her family background in case Dan wanted to delve into areas she'd prefer not to go.

There was a pause while Dan struggled to find the right way to ask his next question. He tried to be tactful…but in the end he just said what was on his mind.

'This Simon, is he Grace's father?'

'No.' Trudi should have expected Dan to have jumped to that conclusion, but she was taken unawares.

'Ah, yes, of course…you told me Grace's father is dead.'

'That's right.'

'So, this Simon, where does he come in?' Dan was determined to break down the wall of silence Trudi had built around her private life. He desperately wanted to know the situation, otherwise how could he start a relationship with her?

She chose her words carefully. 'I knew Simon before I became pregnant with Grace.'

'Were you married to Grace's father?'

'I've never been married.'

Dan hesitated for a moment. Perhaps she has more in common with Jasmine than I imagined. Jasmine Hartley-Browne, the uptown career woman who'd wanted a baby but not a husband. Who'd wanted a baby because it seemed to her to be the fashionable thing to have. Please, prayed Dan silently, don't let this woman be the same.

'Tell me more about Grace's father,' he probed. 'What kind of man was he? Was he a doctor?'

'No.'

'Did you consider getting married once you knew you were having his baby?' Dan persisted.

'Why are you asking so many questions?'

Why, indeed? Dan gulped down the last dregs of his coffee.

'I'd like to know you better, that's all. I'd like to know what your attitude is to certain things—marriage, for instance.'

'Marriage?'

'Yes. Are you in favour of it or not? Speaking personally, I am. Particularly when there are children involved. I just happen to be rather old-fashioned that way. I was only wondering if you felt the same. Obviously you don't.'

'I do believe in marriage,' said Trudi.

'But not enough to marry Grace's father? Or was he married already?' Dan saw the desperate look in her eyes and immediately regretted having asked the last question.

'Sorry,' he said quietly, reaching out and touching her hand.

'Yes, he was married. But it's not what you're thinking.'

Trudi's face had gone white but she was still in control. 'I'm not going to answer any more of those kinds of questions.' She stood up to leave. He held onto her hand.

'Well, I'll ask a different kind of question. Will you have dinner with me one night?'

She hesitated. 'What about Grace?'

'Get a babysitter. People do, you know!'

His hand was still holding hers. The pressure from his strong fingers reinforced the urgency in his voice. His touch was magic, his eyes unwavering as they bored into hers.

'So how about Friday?' he ventured.

'Friday will be fine—on condition I can get a babysitter.' She smiled at Dan, glad he'd persisted.

'Pick you up at eight.'

As they were about to leave, Shelly came rushing up to their table, waving an envelope at Trudi.

'A man came in with this for you.'

'Is it urgent?' asked Trudi, annoyed that Shelly should come bursting in on her lunch with Dan. She was the last person Trudi wanted to pick up any hint of a personal relationship between her and Dan.

'Well, look what it says.' Shelly thrust it at her.

The writing on the envelope said, 'The Hon. Trudi Younghouse'.

'So is that you? The Honourable Trudi

Younghouse?' asked Shelly incredulously. 'Have you got a title? Are you a titled lady, then?'

Damn and blast the girl, seethed Trudi as she took the envelope. She'd deliberately not used her title at the hospital as she didn't want anyone questioning her about it. It always gave people the wrong idea, imagining, like Simon did, that because she was from an aristocratic family she must be very wealthy and was only working for a bit of fun and some pin money.

'Yes, that's me,' she muttered, taking and opening the mystery envelope. It contained a cheque from Simon for £500.

Dan, in the meantime, had moved away and was on his way to his office, but not before he'd heard her admit to having a title.

'Wonders never cease,' said Trudi in surprise. Then, seeing that Shelly's nosiness was still not satisfied, she added, 'It's just some money I was owed by someone.'

As an afterthought, and to herself, she muttered, 'Bet it bounces!'

She was right. It did.

Early on Friday afternoon, Clare walked briskly into Outpatients and headed for Trudi's desk.

Dan's sister wasn't a regular visitor to the department—in fact, Trudi couldn't remember ever having seen her there before. Her job as a phlebotomist usually confined her to the wards, taking blood samples from children who were having treatment or operations. Trudi couldn't imagine why she was now in her territory.

Clare's eyes were sparkling and her face aglow. 'Great news about tonight,' she said conspiratorially.

'Tonight?' Trudi had been too preoccupied with the day's busy flow of patients to think that far ahead.

'You and brother Dan,' enthused Clare. 'Going on a date. Now, be sure to tell me all about it on Monday. I'll catch you at the crèche.'

Trudi was miffed.

'How did you know about that?'

'Ah, well,' Clare said, touching the side of her nose knowingly. 'Dan phoned Jim and asked for suggestions as to where he could take ''someone'' out for a meal. He hasn't been here very long and doesn't know the local eateries, so Jim filled him in. I guessed it must be you he was taking out. Am I right?'

Trudi breathed out heavily. 'Yes. But I don't want it all round the hospital, Clare. You know what a gossipy lot they are here.'

Clare put her finger to her lips. 'Not a word shall I say,' she whispered. 'I'm the very embodiment of discretion.'

'Oh, yes!' Trudi laughed. 'And the Pope's a Muslim!'

'Seriously, I am. You won't get me breathing a word of it.' She narrowed her eyes. 'As long as you spill the beans on Monday!'

She turned to leave and gave a cheery wave. Trudi watched her disappear after giving one final wave and a thumbs-up sign.

'Dan might just as well have taken a full page advert in the *Nursing Times*,' she muttered to herself.

There was something very appealing about Clare which made her blatant nosiness acceptable. Even so, Trudi wished she wouldn't be quite so interested in *her* private affairs.

That evening Trudi fed and bathed Grace a little earlier than usual, hoping she would be well and truly asleep by the time the babysitter arrived from next door. Trinny, Bonzo's owner, had willingly agreed to babysit and was due to turn up in about thirty-five minutes. Just enough time to get ready, she estimated as she stepped into the shower.

A little later, with a couple of minutes to spare, she walked down the stairs of the tiny terraced house and into the downstairs room, glancing at her reflection in the hall mirror as she went past.

She didn't want to admit it, but she'd taken a great deal of effort in creating the right appearance for tonight's date. Not too fancy, not too casual. The filmy black knee-length dress was modestly cut, revealing only the merest hint of bosom. Her freshly washed hair shone like polished copper.

It had been a long time since she'd dressed up for a date. It had been so long ago that she didn't even want to think about it—no point in getting herself depressed.

There was a knock at the door and she let Trinny in. Then Dan arrived and she picked up her coat and walked with him to his car. He looked stunningly handsome in a light grey suit and she was glad she'd dressed up.

'I heard of a place a few miles from here, an old hunting lodge with good food and lots of ambience— oak beams, open fires, antlers on the wall, all that kind of stuff,' he said, starting up the engine. 'Just hope I can find it!'

'Didn't Jim give you directions?' Trudi asked.

'This isn't one of Jim's recommendations,' he said. 'I wasn't going to risk having him and Clare turning up accidentally-on-purpose. The moment I let on that I was taking a woman out I regretted it immediately. Anyway, how did you know I'd spoken to Jim?'

'I had Clare round this afternoon, wanting to confirm it was me you were taking out.'

'Sorry about that.' He touched her hand momentarily between gear changes. 'I do love my sister but she can be a little too intrusive at times. She was married at an early age and she's been trying to get me fixed up for years. She thinks I'm a crusty old bachelor and feels it's her mission in life to get me married as soon as possible. She means well, but it can get a bit tedious.'

The hunting lodge was everything Dan had said it would be—and more. They walked into the sumptuously carpeted and oak-panelled hall and, after giving their names to the girl at Reception, were greeted by the imposing-looking owner who led them through to an equally imposing-looking dining room.

'It's over three hundred years old,' said Dan, quoting from the back of the menu. 'And the place is heaving with ghosts.'

'What kind of ghosts?'

'There's a headless nobleman, a lady in white and a dog.'

'A dog?'

'A Labrador. No one knows for sure but he might have been a Lancaster bomber pilot's pet who pined for his master when he failed to return.'

'That's a bit modern for a ghost, isn't it?'

A cynical tone entered his voice. 'You've got to think of your public when you're running a place like this. Headless Jacobeans are all very well, but it doesn't attract today's youth.'

'I take it you don't believe in all that stuff? Ghosts and everything?'

'I'm more concerned with the living than to waste time frightening myself with ghosts. Life's too short to dwell on the past. What's been has been. That was then, this is now.'

'Couldn't agree more,' said Trudi firmly. Now perhaps he'll stop trying to find out about my past.

Looking around the beautifully appointed dining room, he remarked, 'My parents could never have set foot inside a place like this—unless it was to do the cleaning or lay the carpets. Unlike your family, born with silver spoons in their mouths.'

He said it casually and without malice, but it stung Trudi to the quick. It was precisely to avoid people making those kinds of remarks that she never used her title. She was very annoyed that, because she'd bumped into Simon, he'd given the game away. Probably on purpose.

'I had a posh girlfriend once,' said Dan wickedly, when she didn't rise to the bait. 'She was called Jasmine. Jasmine Hartley-Browne. She spoke a bit like you.'

Trudi felt the colour rise in her cheeks.

'Are you trying to be offensive?'

'Not a bit.' He looked at her with appreciative eyes, his gaze lingering on her breasts. 'Her upper-class accent was one of the sexiest things about her. And there I'm sure the similarity ends. Jasmine was a calculating, hard-bitten, society girl. She had everything and all she wanted from me was a fashion accessory—a baby.'

Trudi froze. What was he saying? Was he trying a new way of getting information out of her…information about her baby?

'A baby as a fashion accessory?' she said. 'Is that what you think Grace is?'

'Oh, good heavens, no!' said Dan. 'Do you think I'd have mentioned Jasmine if I thought for one minute you two were the same?'

'Tell me more about her,' probed Trudi, keen to know more about Dan's former girlfriend. Could she perhaps be a little jealous? Whatever her reasons, she certainly wanted him to tell her about this other woman in his life.

'It was when I was still living in London. I met her at a party. She was very glamorous and I was very flattered, particularly as she so obviously came from a different world to mine. We started to date. She didn't possess a title, like you, but she hinted at her superior family background—superior to mine, that is. It turned her on, she said, going out with me. She kept singing that song about an uptown girl and a downtown guy. It irritated the hell out of me. I felt I was being patronised, but at the same time I was under her spell and so I put up with it. It was only when she suggested that I should give her a child and then disappear from her life that I realised what a dreadful woman she was. Cold, calculating and insulting into the bargain. She just wanted my baby, she didn't want me. "Good lord," she said. "Marry a man with a Yorkshire accent? You must be crazy. What would Mummy and Daddy think? Imagine my children growing up and speaking like you!" I told her to get lost.'

Trudi was shocked.

'I can't believe anyone would say that! What a terrible snob she must have been.'

'I didn't mind too much about that,' admitted Dan. 'I've often been accused of being an inverted snob—just because I speak my mind and call a spade a spade. No, it was the fact that she wanted me as a sperm donor—to give her a baby and then disappear off the scene. My child would have grown up never knowing me as its father.'

As he said the words Trudi flinched. If the surrogacy had gone ahead as planned, Grace wouldn't have known Trudi as her real mother. It would have been Jane who would have brought Grace up, and therefore it would have been Jane who Grace would have known and loved as a mother.

'Jasmine seemed to think that I would just walk away from my child," he continued in disbelief. 'What sort of parent would be able to do that?'

Trudi flinched again, as if he'd slapped her.

He reached out and slid his hand over hers. 'Sorry. This isn't very romantic dinner-table conversation, is it? Let's talk about something else.'

The journey home took longer than she'd remembered it taking to get there.

'You're not going to believe this,' he said after turning up yet another dark country road. 'We're lost.'

'Why shouldn't I believe it? You're new to the area, like I am.'

'It must sound like the oldest trick in the book.'

Dan drove the car onto a verge and killed the engine. Diving into the door's side pocket, he pulled out a road map and switched on the interior car light. After several minutes he satisfied himself that he could find the way back.

'Yep. We're about here,' he said, moving his finger vaguely around the page. Then he turned the car light off and slid his arm around the back of Trudi's seat.

'Maybe I am a bit of a trickster after all,' he said softly, pulling her towards him.

His cheek was against her hair, and he breathed in a fragrance that reminded him of springtime in the Yorkshire Dales and sweet mountain air. He pulled her closer to him and his heart quickened. She looked up at him, her mouth trembling slightly, her lips full and tempting. He kissed her, knowing he'd been longing to do that ever since he'd first seen her. She leaned towards him with her eyes shut and he deepened his kiss, wanting to lose himself in her sweetness.

As he kissed her, she felt his fingertips, stroking between her legs, soft, warm and tormenting, making her burn with desire.

They stayed parked up on the verge for half an hour, kissing like a couple of teenagers. His hands roved over her body, taking her to heights of pleasure she'd never known existed.

Her mind was racing ahead, imagining how wonderful it would be to let him do the one thing her body craved—make love to her.

'We'd better stop,' said Dan with reluctance. 'I can't take much more of this without needing to go very much further. And I'm well past the age of having sex in the car!'

Although she was longing for Dan to make love to her, Trudi was reluctant to start an affair with him so soon. It would mean having to tell him a lot more about herself—a whole lot more—and after the remarks he'd made earlier that suggested he disapproved of surrogacy, she just couldn't face it right now.

She was relieved that he appeared not to want to rush into an affair.

He cupped her face in his hand. 'From the moment I first saw you I knew that you were someone special. I'm not going to spoil it by rushing things. Something as good as this needs to be taken slowly. Do you feel the same?'

Trudi nodded. Dan was a dream come true, a man she could fall madly in love with—if she hadn't done so already. But her joy in knowing him and loving him was tempered by the fact that she feared there could never be a future for them. If he disapproved so strongly about surrogacy, which was how it had very much sounded, how on earth was she ever going to be able to tell him the truth about Grace and her conception?

He started the engine and turned the car round.

They seemed to be driving round half the roads in the county but eventually he pulled up outside her house.

Trudi looked anxiously at her watch in the light from the dashboard. 'Hope the babysitter doesn't bite my head off. I'm an hour later than I said.'

Dan took her to the door, politely turning down her offer of a coffee.

'I'll have a kiss instead,' he said, pulling her towards him. He towered over her as he gathered her to him, pressing his firm, muscular body against the softness of hers.

He seemed to devour her with his lips, caressing her hair with his hands and sliding them hungrily down her pliant body until she moaned in pleasure, arching towards him and clinging to his neck as if her life depended it. It was a long kiss, and afterwards he held her close, wrapped in his strong arms.

'I'll see you in my dreams,' Dan said huskily, reluctantly pulling away. Then he took her latchkey and, pushing open the door, saw her safely inside. He blew a kiss as he walked down the path.

CHAPTER FIVE

'Hı! I thought I'd catch you here.'

Trudi's heart sank when she saw Clare jump out of her car, which had been parked next to her own. She might have known Dan's sister would lie in wait for her in order to conduct a cross-examination about Friday's date.

All day she'd been dreading Clare coming into Outpatients and talking about it in front of the staff. Shelly and Karen had well-tuned antennae which could sense the slightest hint of inter-departmental gossip. A staff sister going out with a consultant was just the kind of juicy morsel they'd love. Dan was well aware of the embarrassment that could be caused if word got out that they were seeing each other out of hospital hours. His sister was a different matter!

'Oh, hi, Clare,' she said, pushing Grace round to the back door of her car.

'Well? How did it go?' asked Clare impatiently.

'Fine. We went to a very nice hunting lodge—can't remember the name—and had a very nice meal.'

'And?'

'And that was it, really. Dan was the perfect gentleman, as you would no doubt expect him to be.'

'But did he say anything about going out again? Are you two now an item?'

'I don't think so.' Trudi was having to choose her words very carefully.

'That brother of mine!' Then Clare had an afterthought. 'You do find him attractive, don't you? I think he's extremely dishy but I'm his adoring little sister and rather prejudiced!'

Trudi couldn't lie. 'He's attractive. Of course he is. But we have to give these things time.' She could have added, And even then there's probably no future for us.

Just as she opened the car door and was about to put Grace in her baby seat, her attention was caught by the squealing of car tyres. She and Clare both looked in the direction of the noise and saw a sporty car stop outside the hospital staff entrance. Shelly, now out of uniform, stepped into the passenger seat of the car which then sped off. Trudi caught a brief glimpse of the driver.

It was Simon. She gasped in shock.

'It's that silly little nurse in your department,' remarked Clare. 'Looks like she's got a new boyfriend. At least she's managed to hook some poor unsuspecting bloke with a flashy car.'

Trudi said nothing. For once she began to feel sorry for Shelly. Far from her new boyfriend being a 'poor unsuspecting bloke', she very much suspected that the young nurse had landed herself with an expert con man.

'Anyway,' said Clare before Trudi could slip into the driver's seat and leave, 'what I really was waiting here for was to ask you to a party on Saturday. Jim's thirtieth.'

'That's very kind of you, Clare. I'll let you know tomorrow if I can get a babysitter.'

'Great,' said Clare, shutting her car door and winding down the window. 'Dan's coming so he can pick you up.' Then, with one of her cheery waves, she was gone.

The next morning, Trudi felt she really had to warn Shelly about getting involved with Simon. She called the nurse into her office.

'Close the door, would you, Shelly?'

Shelly did as she'd been bidden.

'I saw you leave last night. The man who picked you up outside the hospital was Simon, wasn't it?'

Shelly gave a defiant toss of her head and stared at Trudi in sullen silence.

'I know it was him. I'd recognise him anywhere…even in his latest little racing number. I just wanted to warn you about him, Shelly. He's a complete and utter con man.'

This stung the nurse into action. She jumped up. 'You're just jealous! He said you would be. And now you've proved him right!'

'So you talked about me, did you?' Trudi kept her voice low and calm.

'He mentioned you once or twice. It's obvious he would because that's how we met…when he brought the cheque round for you last week.'

'He told you there was a cheque in the envelope, did he?'

'He said it was to repay some money you'd lent him. He always pays his debts, he said.'

'Did he tell you it bounced?'

Shelly's eyes were burning. 'I don't believe you! Simon said you'd say something like that once you found out we were seeing each other.'

'You seemed to have talked about me quite a lot on your one date.'

'Who said it was *one* date? Shelly preened herself. 'We've been out three times and he's mad about me.'

'Fine, Shelly.'

The nurse turned to leave the office.

'We're in love, as a matter of fact. And I won't let anything you say about him put me off.'

'Great. I hope it works out for you. Just one thing, Shelly. Don't lend him any money.'

The contemptuous look that Shelly threw at her as she stomped out of the room only served to make Trudi mutter to herself, 'Well, at least I warned you.'

When Dan picked up Trudi on Saturday evening for Jim's birthday party, he gave her a peck on the cheek and an admiring glance.

'Another stunning outfit, Sister Younghouse? The NHS must be paying you too much!'

'You've a nerve,' she jested. 'Rich consultant like you begrudging a humble nurse a new dress now and then!'

Secretly she was delighted he'd noticed what she was wearing and glad he'd jumped to the conclusion that she'd been spending lots of money on clothes. The truth was, she had no spare cash to spend in dress shops and was now recycling clothes she'd bought in the days before Grace had been conceived. The midnight-blue silk dress had been hanging in her wardrobe for so long she'd needed to have it dry-cleaned before wearing it tonight. She'd slipped it on…and the slinky, silky texture had caressed her body, emphasising her femininity and sensuality.

Dan drove the few miles to his sister's house through country roads that were familiar to Trudi from walks with Grace and Bonzo. They passed through the village where she'd bumped into Dan shortly after her confrontation with Jason's father when she'd found herself temporarily lost. Dan recalled it, too, and as they drove by the post office and general stores he turned to her.

'That's where I picked up a damsel in distress a couple of months back.'

'Nice to be called a damsel.' Trudi laughed. 'I didn't think you counted as a damsel if you'd had a baby!'

'Sometimes I forget that you have.' Dan changed gear as he turned left into another country lane.

'What a strange thing to say,' she remarked.

'When I see you I just see a beautiful young woman. It's hard to believe that slim body of yours has produced a baby.'

'Then you should see my stretch marks!' Trudi said, flattered and embarrassed at the same time.

The car pulled up and joined a line of others parked outside a pretty cottage. Dan switched off the engine and faced her.

'That sounds like an invitation,' he said roguishly.

'What?'

'To see your stretch marks. I'll take a look later if you like. On a purely professional level, you understand.'

The door of the cottage was open and music and

laughter spilled out as they walked up the path. They spotted Clare and Jim among the crowd and made their way through to them.

'Trudi!' shouted Clare above the noise. 'Come and meet the birthday boy. Jim!' she yelled. A bearded man came over to them and was introduced as Clare's husband. Dan handed his brother-in-law a bottle wrapped in shiny paper. Jim pulled the paper down and slapped Dan on the shoulder. 'My favourite port!' he said with glee. Waving the bottle at Clare, he said, 'This isn't for tonight. I'm going to put it safely away.'

'Where are the boys?' enquired Dan, referring to his young nephews.

'Staying overnight with a friend,' assured Clare. 'Now we can make as much noise and behave as badly as we like!'

The party was going with a swing. Food and drink was in abundance but Trudi noticed that Dan was on mineral water after a couple of small beers. She allowed herself just two glasses of wine. Even though she wasn't driving, some basic instinct made her always want to be in control. Perhaps it was her training and the fact that she might be called upon at any time to give medical assistance. Or perhaps it was the memory of the time she'd spent with Simon when, because of his alcoholism, she'd never known when she would need to drive him home—instead of the other way round.

A young man with an earring and shoulder-length red hair was running the disco in a room with the carpet rolled back.

'That's Jim's cousin, Richard,' shouted Clare over

the loud music. 'He's a medical student and does this to pay his way through college.'

'Would you like to dance?' Dan asked Trudi, sweeping her in his arms before she could reply.

He held her close as they moved together on the crowded dance floor. The music's throbbing beat rivalled the hammering of her heart as their bodies pressed together in a sensual swaying motion.

A wave of white heat ran swiftly through her. She could feel the animal warmth of him through his fine cotton shirt. Their bodies moved as one. She knew that if he wanted to stay the night with her she would let him. More than that, she would encourage him to do so. She was so filled with desire for him at that moment she could think of little else.

Her head was in a spin and her emotions were running wild. She wanted Dan like she'd never wanted any man. If there was to be no future for them, then she was prepared to settle for the present. All she knew was that she needed him now.

She pressed her face against the virile roughness of his cheek.

'I was lying about the stretch marks,' she said, deliberately leading him on.

'How am I going to find that out?' he teased. 'Seeing is believing.'

'Mmm,' she confirmed. 'Do you want to stop over tonight, to save driving back into town?' Her meaning was crystal clear.

He hesitated before answering, whirling her frantically round the dance floor. Then he took her by the hand and led her to a corner of the room where it was a little quieter.

'Of course I want to stay with you tonight,' he said thickly, his mouth brushing against her cheek. 'If that's what you want. I told you last week that I didn't want to rush our relationship…and I meant it. But seeing you tonight, holding you, it makes me want more. Makes me want everything. Don't ask me back unless you want the same. I'm past the age when I can put up with playing games.'

'I'm not playing games,' said Trudi. 'I want you as much as you want me.'

He kissed her lightly, cupping her face in his hands. Then he stroked a thumb over her warm, full lips as if priming them for a second onslaught. He brought his mouth down on hers again, this time with passion. A sensation of exquisite pleasure swept over her entire body.

'Let's leave now,' he said with urgency.

'But it's still quite early,' replied Trudi breathlessly. 'We can't really leave yet.'

'The hell we can't!'

He took her hand and they left the room. Grabbing their coats from a pile in the cloakroom, they squeezed their way through the partygoers and out through the front door.

'Shouldn't we say goodbye to Clare and Jim?' asked Trudi, concerned that their early departure might seem a trifle rude.

'What they don't know they won't worry about,' said Dan, opening the car's passenger door and guiding her in.

They drove at a sedate speed, Dan constantly keeping an eye on the speedometer.

'Don't want to get stopped for speeding,' he said.

'I don't think I can use the doctor on call excuse when I've got a sexy young woman in the seat next to me. The cops wouldn't be taken in by that, I'm sure.'

They rounded a bend and, as if he'd had a premonition, they found themselves stopped by a police road block. Lights were flashing, police officers and paramedics were milling around. It was obvious there'd been a serious road traffic accident.

Dan wound down his window as a policeman approached.

'Can you turn round, sir, and make a detour through the next village? This road is blocked. There's been a bad accident.'

'Can we do anything to help, officer?' Dan asked. 'I'm a doctor and my companion is a nurse.'

'That's very good of you, sir, but the injured parties have been transferred to hospital. We're just in the process of clearing up and waiting for the low-loader to come and remove the vehicles.'

'What happened?' asked Dan and Trudi in unison.

'Two young couples going too fast on these narrow roads, basically. One couple on a motorbike, another couple in a car. From what they said, it seems they were having some kind of race. Whatever it was they were having, the couple on the motorbike came off worse. Much worse. They've just been taken to hospital.'

'What about the other couple? Are they injured?'

'Not badly. Just very shaken. They're in the back of a police vehicle and refuse to go to hospital. The paramedics gave them a quick once-over.' The police officer paused, then said, 'As you're a doctor, it wouldn't be a bad idea if you came and talked to them, just to make sure they're all right before we take them to the police station.'

Dan and Trudi got out of the car and, after picking up Dan's doctor's bag, followed the officer over to one of the police cars. They walked past the mangled wreckage of the motorbike and sports car which was strewn across the centre of the road.

'It's a wonder anyone got out of that alive,' Dan remarked to the officer.

'They make cars stronger than they used to. With crumple zones and airbags and God knows what else. Motorbikes are a different matter altogether. If you're knocked off one of those you're looking at major injuries, if not death.'

'How were the couple on the bike?' asked Dan.

'Not good. Not good at all. Particularly the young man.'

As they approached the police car they came across three or four other officers. One was holding an intoximeter machine. Some kind of argument was going on between the people in the car and an officer.

'What's up?' asked the policeman with Dan and Trudi.

'The man refuses to give a specimen of breath. I can smell alcohol on him but he swears he wasn't the driver…says it was the girl. She's given a breath test and that was clear.'

Trudi was close enough to the police car to look at the young couple sitting in the back. The man had his arm around the girl, who was sobbing. In the flashing blue light Trudi recognised them.

It was Simon and Shelly.

'We know them!' she said in shocked dismay to an officer standing near the car. Turning to Dan, she said in distress, 'It's Simon and Shelly. Shelly's one of the nurses in my department.'

Dan peered into the back seat for confirmation. 'And Simon is…is the man I saw with you at the supermarket.'

'Yes. I just can't believe it.'

'Did you say his name was Simon?' remarked the officer, checking his notebook. 'He told us it was Ben.'

'I wonder why he would say that?' puzzled Trudi.

'We've a good idea,' said the officer, nodding to his companion with the intoximeter. 'You'd be surprised how many people involved in road accidents or drink-driving give false names. We're taking them both back to the police station when the van comes so they can give full statements.'

'We'd like to give them that quick examination first,' Dan said to the officer who had first spoken to them.

'Sure thing, Doc,' he said, opening the car door. Shelly and Simon looked up and saw the two medics.

'Oh, Trudi,' sobbed Shelly. 'I'm so glad to see you! It's been awful… I'm so worried about Karen and Kev!'

'Karen and Kev were the couple on the motor-bike?' Trudi had suspected as much but had dreaded finding out if it was true. Especially as she now knew they had serious injuries.

Shelly pulled away from Simon and tried to get out of the car to speak to Trudi. Simon held onto her arm.

'Remember what we said—don't go blabbing.' His tone was quiet but threatening.

Shelly pulled away and stepped out of the police car. She was shaking.

Trudi put a comforting arm around her. 'You've had a bad shock. A very bad shock. Just lean on me for a while. Do you hurt anywhere? Your neck or chest or legs? Any bleeding?'

Shelly shook her head. 'No,' she whimpered. 'The ambulance crew checked us over. Said we might have whiplash pains tomorrow. When I told them I was a nurse they seemed to think I could take care of myself.'

'They would assume you'd know whether or not you needed further medical attention, which is a fair assumption. You're very shaken but are you in shock, do you think?' asked Trudi, concerned also that Shelly might be suffering from internal crush injuries.

'I'm pretty sure I'm not,' said the nurse, reacting positively to Trudi's calm questioning.

Trudi put a hand on Shelly's forehead. 'Your skin feels fine, not cold and clammy,' she said reassuringly. 'And you don't appear to be sweating. Any sickness or giddiness?'

'No.'

Trudi slipped her fingers down the girl's wrist and held them there for a few moments.

'Your pulse is racing… That's not surprising under the circumstances, but you don't seem to be hyperventilating. Are you thirsty?'

Shelly shook her head.

'Feeling sick?'

'I did at first, after seeing how bad Karen and Kev were. We did our best for them until the ambulance arrived—tried to stop the bleeding and put them in the recovery position and—'

'So what's all this about "Ben"?' Trudi asked, looking over to the police car where Dan had moved into the seat next to Simon and was presumably also checking him for symptoms of shock and internal injury.

'Him!' the nurse said scornfully between sobs. Then, seeing the police officers nearby, she held her tongue.

'Were you really driving the car, Shelly?' she asked quietly, out of earshot of the police.

'I'm not saying anything. I'm saying nothing at all. It's none of your business.'

Trudi sighed resignedly. It was back to the old defiant Shelly once again.

At that moment another police vehicle arrived, a large police van.

'We're going to take these two back to the police station to get their statements,' said the officer who had been holding the intoximeter.

Shelly seemed to lose her nerve again on hearing this and clutched at Trudi.

'Will you come with me? *Please*.' The terrified look in her eyes gave Trudi little alternative.

Simon and Shelly were escorted to the police van and Dan and Trudi returned to their car, having agreed to follow them to the police station.

'What about your babysitter?' asked Dan.

'I'd better ring her.' Trudi phoned from Dan's mobile as they headed into town, following the van.

Dan heard only one side of the conversation but presumed that everything was sorted out.

'No problems?' he asked when she switched off the phone.

'Trinny says she'll stay overnight in the spare bed. Then I won't be worried about how late we get back.'

At the police station Simon was taken into one interview room, Shelly into another. Trudi and Dan sat in the main office and waited.

'Would you like to contact your solicitor?' Shelly was asked by the officer conducting the taped interview.

'Don't think so,' said Shelly with false courage. 'I can manage on my own. Anyway, I haven't got a solicitor. Never needed one.'

'It's your right to have one present if you wish,' said the officer. 'I must warn you that you could be facing serious charges.'

'Serious charges? Like what?' Shelly was back to her old cheeky ways. 'I've done nothing wrong. I've not been drinking.'

'That's true. Your breath test was negative. But, depending on the evidence, you could be facing a charge of dangerous driving.'

Shelly blanched.

'You *were* the driver of the vehicle, I take it?'

Shelly's mouth tensed and she didn't reply.

'At the scene of the accident your companion said that you were the driver.'

'He did say that, yes.'

'So, were you the driver of the vehicle?' persisted the officer.

Shelly cast a nervous glance over her shoulder towards the back of the room where a woman police constable was sitting on a hard wooden chair.

'Yes,' she answered.

The police officer knew she was lying. His pager buzzed. 'I'm stopping the tape and will be back in a few moments,' he said, leaving Shelly and the constable alone in the room.

While he was gone neither of them spoke a word. The officer was back within three minutes.

'I've just heard from a police colleague at the hospital. The couple on the motorbike are in Intensive Care. The young man isn't expected to survive.'

Shelly uttered a cry and buried her head in her hands.

'So you see, miss, as the driver of the vehicle you could be facing very serious charges. I'm talking about causing death by dangerous driving. You could be looking at a long prison term.'

All the colour drained from her face. 'Oh, no… Oh, no…' she kept repeating. 'Don't let Kev and Karen die. We didn't mean any harm… It was just a game… We didn't mean to hit them!'

'You mean *you* didn't mean to hit them,' corrected the officer, who announced he was starting the recording again. 'You admitted earlier that you were driving the car. That is right, isn't it?'

All the girl's bravado disappeared and she crumpled up in the chair, sobbing her heart out.

'Do you want a glass of water?' asked the woman constable. Shelly shook her head.

The officer spoke into the tape recorder. 'I'm stopping this recording at twelve thirty-six a.m.'

When Shelly had been left to cry for a few minutes, he spoke kindly to her.

'It wasn't you driving, love, was it?'

Shelly shook her head.

'It was that creep in the other room…the one who stinks of drink. I don't know why you're shielding him. Why should you take the rap for him?' The officer looked down at his notepad. 'Ben, is it? I think you should tell me the truth and let this Ben get charged instead. We'll throw the book at him— dangerous driving, refusing to give a specimen of breath…and quite probably causing death by dangerous driving…'

'Simon,' said Shelly who'd managed to pull herself together. 'His name's Simon, not Ben.'

'Well, there you go,' said the officer. 'Giving a false name as well! We'll also have him for obstructing a police officer and attempting to pervert the course of justice. And if he thinks he's getting bail tonight he's got another think coming!'

CHAPTER SIX

INSTEAD of Dan staying the night with Trudi, Shelly did. Trudi took pity on the young nurse and realised she was in no state to go home on her own.

'Do you live with your parents, Shelly?'

'No, I've got a flat in town. I'll be all right.'

'You're coming back with me. I've got a spare bed that I can make up in a trice.'

Then she remembered. 'Ah, the babysitter's in that one. Never mind, you can have my bed and I'll sleep on the couch.'

Shelly was overcome with Trudi's generous offer. 'You're so kind,' she said, wiping away an emotional teardrop. 'I don't know why you're being so nice to me.'

The next morning, Sunday, Trinny crept quietly down the stairs to let herself out. She was startled to see Trudi on the couch with a duvet pulled up to her chin.

'It's a long story,' she muttered drowsily in response to Trinny's raised eyebrows.

'Tell me later,' Trinny whispered conspiratorially. 'Grace was as good as gold last night and was still asleep when I popped my head round the nursery door just now.'

'Thanks, Trinny,' said Trudi hoarsely.

'Any time,' replied the babysitter as she let herself out.

Now that she was awake she may as well get up, Trudi decided. With a sinking heart she remembered that Shelly was still upstairs and that she was probably lumbered with the girl for several more hours.

The weekends were precious to Trudi. It was the only quality time she was able to spend with Grace—and now it looked as if she'd be sharing their day with Shelly, one of the most unpleasant young women she'd ever come across.

Then there was Karen to think of as well.

Before doing anything, before she even made herself a coffee, she was on the phone to the County General where the police had told her Karen and Kev had been taken.

'Intensive Care, please,' she told the operator.

When she was put through to the ICU she enquired first about Karen.

'Are you a relative?' asked the sister in charge.

'No, but I'm a staff sister at Highfield Children's Hospital where Karen works. She's a nurse in my department and I'm very anxious to know how she is after the accident.'

'She's doing fine. We're going to move her to a recovery ward when the trauma specialist has given her a final check-over. Fortunately, her injuries are mostly superficial.'

'That's wonderful!' Trudi was immensely relieved. After what the police had told her the previous night, she'd been expecting Karen to be on a life-support machine at the very least. Then she re-

Play The *Lucky Hearts* Game

and get...
FREE BOOKS & a FREE GIFT...
YOURS to KEEP!

Yes! I have scratched off the silver card. Please send me my **FREE BOOKS** and **FREE MYSTERY GIFT**. I understand that I am under no obligation to purchase any books as explained on the back of this card. I am over 18 years of age.

Scratch Here! then look below to see what you can claim...

M1CI

Ms/Mrs/Miss/Mr _____ Initials _____

BLOCK CAPITALS PLEASE

Surname _____

Address _____

_____

Postcode _____

Twenty-one gets you
4 FREE BOOKS and a
MYSTERY GIFT!

Twenty gets you
2 FREE BOOKS and a
MYSTERY GIFT!

Nineteen gets you
2 FREE BOOKS!

TRY AGAIN!

NO STAMP NEEDED!

MILLS & BOON READER SERVICE
FREE BOOK OFFER
FREEPOST CN81
CROYDON
CR9 3WZ

NO STAMP
NECESSARY
IF POSTED IN
THE U.K. OR N.I.

membered what the desk sergeant had said about Kev—that he wasn't expected to survive…

'What about the young man, Kev?' she asked, involuntarily holding her breath.

'He's still in the operating theatre. His parents have been informed and are on their way. That's all I can tell you.'

Trudi thanked her and put down the phone with a heavy heart. She'd never actually met the famous Kev but felt she knew him intimately from the constant stream of details fed by Karen to anyone who happened to be in earshot. Mostly, she believed, it was to impress Shelly who, although by far the more attractive-looking, seemed to have trouble in catching a man.

And wasn't that the reason surgeons were at the moment fighting for Kev's life? All because Shelly had needed a boyfriend so badly she'd let herself be taken in by the unscrupulous Simon. But, then, who was she to criticise? Hadn't she also been taken in by him? A good-looking, smooth operator like Simon was going to make conquests whenever and wherever he pleased.

Trudi shuddered and realised how lucky she was to have got rid of him before he'd involved her in a tragedy through his irresponsible, excessive drinking. All she'd lost had been her pride, a little confidence and five hundred pounds. Cheap at the price.

Trudi didn't feel like a coffee now. Instead, she made her way up to Grace's room. The baby was lying on her back, her large blue eyes gazing at the door. When Trudi went to her she gave a whoop of delight and started kicking her legs with excitement.

It was one of the best moments in the day for Trudi as she picked up her baby and held her close to her heart.

'You're a little sweetie, aren't you?' she said, cuddling her for a moment before laying her down on the changing mat. She exchanged Grace's wet nappy for a dry one and then carried her downstairs for her morning feed.

As she cradled Grace in her arms, watching her suck vigorously at the bottle, Trudi felt a pang of regret. Regret that she hadn't breast-fed her baby. She sighed. Now that Grace was nearly nine months old she would most likely have been on a bottle anyway, she told herself. But she would have liked to have given her the best start in life—and breast-feeding, if the mother was healthy, Trudi had always considered to be the best for a baby. Good for the mother, too, she also believed. It was, after all, the natural thing to do. Of course she'd made herself put all that to the back of her mind during her pregnancy. All she'd known had been that because she'd agreed to give this baby to her sister at birth, there had been no point in even considering breast-feeding. By the time the circumstances had changed and she was keeping the baby, she'd convinced herself that bottle-feeding Grace had still been the best option. Her emotions had been erratic and the shock of her sister's death had caused her to have problems providing breast milk.

As it was, when she'd been asked by the midwife if she was planning on breast-feeding, she'd automatically said no, and that had been that. Grace had been put on a bottle and had thrived on it.

Looking down at her now, her bonny face, her clear skin and bright, shining eyes, she was the picture of health. The baby didn't appear to have suffered by not having been breast-fed, she conceded. But Trudi felt that, as a mother, *she* had.

'I'll breast-feed the next one,' Trudi said out loud. The next one? What was she thinking of? There wasn't going to be another baby.

How could she possibly get herself involved with a man of integrity, the only kind of man with whom she wanted a lifelong relationship? Any man of worth was bound to find out the truth about her and may even despise her for it.

Bitter tears stung her eyes. Not only had fate cheated her out of breast-feeding her baby, it had robbed her of a future with a man of principle. A man like Dan, for instance. She only had to recall the look on his face when they'd talked about what had happened with his relationship with Jasmine. Of course, the circumstances had been different—but it didn't alter the fact that he might despise the whole idea. How on earth could she tell him that she'd been involved with surrogacy? She didn't want to risk losing him.

Her sad reflections were interrupted by the sound of footsteps on the stairs. Shelly appeared in the room.

'Did you sleep well?' Trudi asked the bedraggled-looking girl.

'Sort of. At least I don't remember waking up until now.'

Glancing across at the couch with the duvet still

piled up on it, she recalled in a rush where Trudi had spent the night.

'I'm so sorry I pushed you out of your bed. You should have let me sleep down here.'

'Wouldn't have dreamed of it,' replied Trudi, pleased that Shelly was at least showing a little gratitude. 'By the way, I phoned the hospital and Karen's out of danger.'

Shelly clutched a kitchen chair to steady herself. 'Thank God,' she breathed. 'And Kev?'

'They wouldn't tell me much. Just that he was still in the operating theatre and that his parents were on the way.'

Shelly pulled out the chair and sat down heavily, leaning her elbows on the scrubbed pine table. Slowly she lowered her head into her hands.

'It's a nightmare. Tell me I'm dreaming. Say it isn't true about last night.'

'I'm afraid it is. But you know what they say— where there's life, there's hope. And Kev is still alive.'

Later that morning, Trudi went next door to ask Trinny if she'd mind looking after Grace for an hour while they went to visit Karen at the hospital.

Trudi told her neighbour the story of the previous night's accident and the reason she'd given up her bed to her nursing colleague.

'And I thought you might be bringing back that handsome doctor friend of yours!'

'Whatever gave you that idea?' said Trudi innocently.

'The adoring way you looked at him, and the

equally lustful way he couldn't take his eyes off you!'

Trudi didn't trust herself to say anything and just handed Grace over.

'Another time, maybe.' Trinny took the baby and cuddled her. 'Take your time at the hospital, no need to rush back. It's a treat for me to look after such a gorgeous baby!'

At the hospital Trudi and Shelly were directed to Karen's ward, which seemed to be miles away, up two flights of stairs and along endless corridors. In comparison with Highfield, the large general hospital was very large indeed.

Karen was in a six-bed ward and was sitting up and flicking through a magazine when they walked in. Shelly rushed up to her and blurted out emotionally, 'Oh, Karen, I'm sorry!'

Karen was delighted to see them and made a brave effort at smiling. Her face was a mass of cuts and bruises, there were sutures in a couple of places and her cheeks, nose and chin were stained yellow with antiseptic. She was recognisable, but only just.

They sat on visitors' chairs on either side of her bed and Karen assured them that she was fine.

'They've told me I won't have any permanent scars or anything. The crash helmet saved me really. They've said I was very lucky.'

'Let's hope Kev is lucky as well,' said Shelly, who regretted them the moment she'd got the words out.

Trudi took a deep breath. 'We heard he'd been operated on last night,' she said, trying to make it sound positive.

'Yeah,' said Karen, clutching her hands together. 'They told me he'd had a successful operation and that I wasn't to worry. But I can't help worrying. I want to go and see him but they won't let me. Probably because I'm a bit wobbly on my feet at the moment. They could take me in a wheelchair, I suppose, but I expect they're short-staffed like we are at Highfield.'

It was obvious that Karen had no idea how seriously injured her boyfriend was…that his life was hanging in the balance.

'I asked about Kev at Reception just now,' said Trudi, trying to keep her voice noncommittal. 'They rang through to the ward and said that Kev's parents were with him.'

'Oh, good,' said Karen. 'At least he's got someone to talk to.'

Trudi couldn't look her in the eye. What she and Shelly both knew was that he wasn't talking to anyone, not even his parents. Kev was unconscious. His parents were watching and waiting in the hope that their son would soon pull out of his coma.

'The next twenty-four hours are crucial,' the nurse had told Trudi when she'd enquired about the prognosis.

She wasn't going to mention that to Karen. There was no point in burdening the girl with extra worries when she needed all her strength to recover fully herself. Karen would find out soon enough if there was going to be some really bad news.

Trudi drove Shelly home to her flat in town after the brief hospital visit. The girl was adamant that she was now sufficiently over the shock of the accident to be on her own. She did hint that she might phone her parents and go and stay with them for a few days.

'What about work? Won't I be letting you down if I don't come in?' she asked, showing uncharacteristic concern for others.

'Don't worry about that,' reassured Trudi. 'I certainly wasn't expecting you to turn up for work tomorrow.'

'Karen won't be there either,' reminded Shelly.

'I'd already thought of that and I'd planned to speak to Human Resources at Highfield to arrange for agency cover for the two of you.'

Trudi waved Shelly off at the door of her apartment block and breathed a sigh of relief. Though the nurse had changed her attitude beyond recognition in the past twenty-four hours, it would be too much to hope that the change might be permanent. She was glad the girl hadn't suffered any long-term harm from the accident…but she was also relieved that she wouldn't be seeing her at work for the next few days.

She hated to admit it, but Shelly's constant sniping and successive attempts at troublemaking were beginning to get through to her. Instead of looking forward to the day's work, she found herself dreading going in. At first she'd thought it had been because she'd hated leaving Grace—but that was something she was now becoming used to and it didn't upset her the way it once had. No, it was the unpleasant working atmosphere, caused mainly by Shelly, that added to the normal amount of stress to be expected in a busy outpatients department.

When Monday morning came, it was like working in a different hospital.

The two agency nurse replacements for Karen and Shelly were older women who'd returned to work after their families had grown up. Stella and Joan were solid, down-to-earth and very competent nurses. In their capable hands the outpatients department started to run like a well-oiled machine in a manner often envisaged by Trudi but rarely achieved.

In the afternoon, during a lull in the workload, Trudi was having a coffee with them both and complimented them on the good job they'd done.

'You get used to having to hit the ground running each time you start a new job,' said Joan. 'Doing agency work teaches you that much at least! You know that you've no time to ease yourself into it gently because you're usually called out when there's some sort of emergency and you're needed to fill in at short notice.'

Stella agreed. 'It's quite a challenge, never knowing what kind of nursing you're going to be doing from one week to the next. Sometimes you get to stay quite a long time in a particular hospital and then you get to know your workmates and the patients better.'

'I was lucky in that respect,' said Trudi. 'I did agency work for a few months before my baby was born and I was sent to this hospital for most of that time. Not in this particular department, though. I wasn't too bothered about having a nine-to-five job like I am now. Then I was able to do all the different nursing shifts.'

'You've got a baby, have you? Boy or girl?'

'Little girl, nearly nine months old.'

'That's nice. What do you do with her when you're at work? Does your mum look after her?'

'I'm afraid both my parents are dead,' replied Trudi. 'But there are marvellous crèche facilities at the hospital so she's well looked after.'

'That's handy,' Stella enthused. 'There was none of that when I had my kids. You were just expected to stay at home at look after them yourself.'

'That's true,' agreed Joan. 'My mum was happy to mind the first baby, but when I had three more, including twins, that was the end of that! I just had to give up work and look after them myself.'

'Me, too,' said Stella. 'Still, they grow up so quickly. I don't regret spending time at home when they were young.'

'Me neither,' rejoined Joan. 'Though it would have been nice to have been given the choice.'

Trudi felt a pang of envy. How she wished she'd been able to choose between working or staying at home. She'd found it so hard to leave Grace at the crèche when she'd started this job. She knew that, given the choice, she'd have chosen to stay at home for at least a couple of years after the birth of the baby. She was only too aware of how quickly time was passing and that she was missing out on all those irreplaceable days of Grace's babyhood.

Two hours later, on her way to collect her from the crèche, Trudi bumped into Dan.

'Thought I'd find you here,' he said. 'Just wanted to know if everything's OK with you?'

'I'm fine, thanks.' Trudi experienced the familiar warm glow that filled her whenever Dan was near.

'What's the news about the accident victims?'

'I phoned County General at lunchtime and spoke to Karen for a few minutes. She's progressing well. Kev's situation hasn't changed. He's still in the ICU with his parents at his bedside. I think Karen's now aware of how finely balanced things are with him, which she wasn't before. She was quite weepy on the phone.'

'And Shelly. Is she still staying with you?'

'I took her home yesterday. She's taking some sick leave and won't be back for a few days. We've got two terrific agency nurses in the department now and I'm very loath to let them go. I spoke to Human Resources and suggested that when Shelly and Karen return they're put in different departments. For their own sakes, really, as well as mine!'

'That Shelly's certainly a little minx. I'll make sure she's not put anywhere near my wards.'

Trudi was aware that they were each trying to prolong the conversation…looking for an excuse to remain standing close to each other.

Dan glanced quickly at his watch. 'Not quite time for ward rounds.'

'It was a good party on Saturday,' she said in an attempt to keep him longer.

'The little bit of it we saw,' Dan remarked, smiling. 'We left quite early, if you remember…to inspect some so-called stretch marks.'

Trudi blushed at the memory. 'Oh, yes. So we did. It seems so long ago now. So much has happened since—the accident and everything.'

'I was just wondering,' he ventured, 'if you're not doing anything this Saturday, would you like to help me mind Clare's brood for the day? She and Jim have been invited to a wedding and I volunteered to do the kindly uncle act and look after the boys. Now it's getting close to the event I'm not so sure I can cope with three small children on my own!'

'You'd cope, I'm sure,' replied Trudi, secretly delighted that he'd asked. 'You're so good with your child patients. They all adore you!'

'Being a paediatric cardiologist is quite a different matter from actually coping single-handed with small kids. I'm well aware that without the nursing staff to give me support and back-up, my job would be impossible. Here at the hospital I give orders and others carry them out—they're the ones who do the actual caring for the children and babies. As I told you in the supermarket, my experience of babies is very limited. I've never changed a nappy in my life!'

'I'll come and show you how to do it, then,' said Trudi with a laugh. 'But I'm sure Clare wouldn't have asked you to mind the children if she didn't think you could cope.'

'It's probably just another of her ploys to get me married and into fatherhood as quickly as possible.'

'Either that or she wants to put you off completely! Well, I'd love to come. It will be nice for Grace as well. She'll know Clare's youngest two from the crèche. That is, if little ones of nine months old recognise anyone apart from those who feed them.' She reluctantly turned to walk away. 'I must go and pick her up now or I'll be late.'

'See you,' said Dan, leaving for his ward round. His step was lighter and he found it hard to wipe the grin off his face. Trudi always had that effect on him, making him feel happy and bright and years younger.

He was glad Clare had suggested asking Trudi to come along on Saturday to help with the children. He wasn't going to mention that, of course…he'd much rather Trudi believed it had been his idea.

CHAPTER SEVEN

AN UNFAMILIAR car pulled up outside Trudi's house on the Saturday morning. It was large and dark blue with three rows of seats. She was surprised to see Dan get out and walk up the path.

'New car?' she enquired.

'No. I've swapped with Jim. He's going to take mine to the wedding instead of Clare's old banger so he can leave me his "people carrier" for the kids. It's got all the straps and baby seats and all that stuff.'

He helped her carry Grace's paraphernalia—spare clothes, nappies, feeding bottles, changing mat and folded pushchair—out to the car. Trudi strapped Grace into one of the baby seats before going back to the house to check that she'd remembered everything. Then she locked up.

As she slid into the passenger seat Dan gave her an admiring glance. 'I hadn't realised what a big production it is, going out for a few hours with a baby. You've brought everything apart from the kitchen sink. Do you have to do this every day when you take her to the crèche?'

Trudi nodded. 'It's become second nature to me now. I've got it down to a fine art and can be out of the house, all packed up and in the car in three minutes.'

'You've timed it?' Dan laughed as he started the engine.

She also laughed. 'Well, you may as well make a game out of it! It's something I had to get used to and now I can do it with my eyes closed.'

Trudi snuggled into the car seat, feeling relaxed and happy. Normally she'd have resented having to go through the rushed weekday morning routine at a weekend. But it was different today. The anticipation of spending a whole day with Dan filled her with the kind of tingling excitement she remembered from childhood at the approach of a birthday or Christmas.

As they arrived at his sister's house the whole family was waiting outside for them. Clare and Jim were dressed up to the nines, standing next to two young boys who were jumping up and down, yelling at the tops of their voices, 'Uncle Dan! Uncle Dan!' Jack, the youngest, was doing his best to jump up and down in his father's arms, joining in the chorus of enthusiastic welcome.

'Somebody's popular round here!' remarked Trudi.

'Only because I spoil them rotten.' Dan got out and helped Trudi unload Grace and her belongings. They were instantly mobbed by the two older boys.

'Hey, let me get into the house, you two!'

'Uncle Dan! Uncle Dan!' they screamed, almost hysterical with excitement.

'Hope you don't mind helping to look after my kids while Jim and I escape for the day,' Clare asked Trudi.

'Not at all,' she replied sincerely. 'They're great!'

She cast envious eyes on the three youngsters,

imagining how nice it would be to look forward to having three children herself. Seeing them all together, bursting with exuberant energy, she realised with sadness what a different kind of childhood her own baby would have, being an only child. No brothers or sisters to grow up with. Poor Grace!

'This is Callum who's nearly two, Jack is one year old—but, of course, you and Grace know them from the hospital crèche, don't you? And this is Liam who's three—'

'Free and a *half*!' interrupted their oldest son.

The introductions made, Jim and Clare left quickly for the wedding. A day on their own without the children was a rare treat and they wanted to relish every moment of it.

'See you tomorrow,' Jim said as he handed Jack to Dan. Trudi overheard. Was Jim talking to his baby son or to Dan?

'Tomorrow?' she said to Dan as they waved them off.

'They're staying overnight in Norwich,' he said. 'That's where the reception is and the hotel was offering a special room price for the wedding guests. I'm sleeping here tonight.' He shot her a look. 'Of course I'll take you and Grace home before the children's bedtime.' A pause. 'If that's what you want.'

Before she could answer, he turned and walked with Jack into the house, followed by his adoring nephews.

It was some minutes before the boys even noticed Trudi and Grace—or perhaps they were deliberately avoiding looking at her. After all, here was someone with another baby who might take their uncle's precious attention away from them. She was hoping they weren't resenting her being there.

She needn't have worried. Once Dan had put Jack down on the carpeted floor next to Grace, the two other boys turned their attention to her.

'This is Trudi,' Dan told them.

'Is she your girlfriend?' Liam asked boldly.

'I suppose she is,' Dan replied without looking at her.

Out of the corner of her eye Trudi could see that Callum, holding a wooden brick, was toddling towards the spot where Grace was lying on the floor. The baby was kicking her legs and gurgling but was in imminent danger of being clobbered, either deliberately or accidentally, by the two-year-old. She rushed over and picked her up, putting her in the playpen for protection.

'You need eyes in the back of your head around here,' said Dan.

'I'm sure Callum's only being friendly, but I'm not taking any chances. He looks a bit mischievous, particularly with that brick in his hand!'

'Can we go to the park, Uncle Dan?' pleaded Liam.

'Park! Park! Park!' added Callum for extra emphasis.

Even little Jack, who'd managed to pull himself up to a standing position by using a chair, made a brave attempt at saying, 'Park.'

'That's a good idea,' said Dan. 'Hands up all those who want to go to the park.'

'Me! Me! Me!'

Three pairs of little hands waved in the air and

baby Jack lost his balance and landed on the floor with a bump. Trudi was impressed that he didn't cry but just startled crawling towards another chair and another attempt at standing up. Being the youngest of three, it made you tough!

They set off to the park, which was a ten-minute walk away. Jack and Callum were secured in the double pushchair and Grace was put in her own stroller. Liam had taken a shine to Trudi and insisted on walking next to her so he could point out the various landmarks and items of interest along the route.

'My nursery school is down there,' he said importantly. 'And this is where a big dog barks behind the gate. Mummy says he won't come out and bite us. He only bites bad people who are trying to steal fings.'

Further along the road there was another important pronouncement from Liam.

'This is where I dropped my ice cream and Mummy said I couldn't pick it up again.'

'Why was that?'

'I don't know. It only had a tiny bit of mud on it. And the dog that ate it didn't mind the mud…so it would probably have been all right, wouldn't it?'

'I think your mummy was right, Liam. It's better not to eat things that have fallen on the floor.'

'Because of Germans?'

Trudi hid a smile. 'Germs, I think she meant. Because of germs.'

'Are you a nurse like my mummy?' asked two-year-old Callum, joining in the conversation.

'Yes, I am.'

'I want to be a nurse when I'm big,' he said with conviction.

'When I grow up I'm going to be a doctor like Uncle Dan,' decided Liam. 'Then I'd have a big black bag to take with me everywhere.' He pointed to Dan's ever-present doctor's bag which was stuffed in the shopping compartment of the double push-chair.

Dan smirked on hearing this. 'So much for inspiring the younger generation with vocations to heal the sick when all they really yearn for is the bag! Hey, Liam, you could be a plumber. They've got even bigger bags than doctors!'

Liam was thoughtful. 'Yes, I might be a plumber.' Looking up at Trudi, he asked, 'What's a plumber?'

As she explained the intricacies of plumbing—all the pipes and the water—she could see that medicine was going to be taking second place in Liam's choice of careers from now on.

At the park the play area was a hive of activity. Youngsters and their parents were enjoying the delights of the swings, roundabouts and climbing frames.

Trudi found space on a nearby bench and sat down with Grace and Jack while Dan took the two older boys to the swings. They looked like a real family, a mum and dad with four happy children, thought Trudi wistfully as she hugged the two little ones to her. The woman seated next to her must have thought the same thing.

'You and your husband have certainly got your hands full,' she commented in a friendly manner. 'Are the two youngest twins?'

'No,' answered Trudi regretfully. 'And only one of the children is mine. The others belong to a friend.' She let the remark about 'your husband' pass. A park bench was no place to be discussing one's domestic arrangements with a complete stranger. If the woman believed that Dan was her husband, well, why not let her? It felt good to Trudi, hearing him described as such.

They started chatting, as mothers of young children did.

'Your little girl's got gorgeous red hair,' said Trudi, admiring the curly-headed toddler playing at her feet.

'It's a boy, actually,' said the woman, grinning broadly. 'I just can't bear to cut his curls, so I'm afraid he does look like a girl! When he goes to nursery school I'll probably have to cut them off or else he might get teased.' She ran her hand lovingly over the flaming red curls. 'And when he gets older he'll probably hate all these curls. Shame, isn't it? They're wasted on him really.'

Trudi agreed. 'Do you have any other children?'

'A little girl of four,' she replied. 'She's over there in the playhouse. Unfortunately she's taken after me and has dead straight mousy hair!'

As if on cue, a small girl in a bright yellow T-shirt and denim shorts came running out of the playhouse towards them. She was crying.

'Oh, dear,' said her mother resignedly. 'Looks like someone's hit her! Children can be little beasts to each other, can't they?' The woman waited for the child to reach her.

'What's the matter, Abigail? Did somebody hurt you?'

The child didn't answer but continued to cry almost hysterically.

'I can't kiss it better if you won't tell me what's the matter,' reasoned her mother as she hugged the child to her.

Strangely, the child pulled away from her mother's embrace and lay down on the ground, screaming.

'Whatever's the matter, Abigail?' she asked. Turning to Trudi, she said, almost in embarrassment, 'She's not normally like this. She's never thrown a tantrum in her life.'

Eventually the child calmed down a little and they could make out the words, 'Bee! Bee!'

'Oh,' said her mother sympathetically, 'I'll bet she's been stung by a bee. She had a nasty bee sting last year and I had to get something from the chemist to make her arm go down. It was all puffy.'

'Bee stung me on my arm again,' said the child between sobs.

'I think we'd better go home,' said her mother, putting Abigail's baby brother in his pushchair in readiness. 'I've still got some of that antihistamine cream and that will do the trick. Come on, Abigail, get up, there's a good girl. I know it hurts but we'll soon have it sorted out for you. Mummy will make it better.'

The woman went to her daughter and looked at her left arm. It was obvious where she'd been stung because the upper arm, just below the T-shirt sleeve, was very swollen and red.

'If it's a bee sting it may still be in her arm,' said

Trudi, putting the two children in their pushchairs and going over to where the now quiet Abigail was lying.

She examined the child's swollen arm but couldn't immediately see the sting with its poisonous sac.

'She's probably rubbed it off,' said Trudi. Then she found the small sting, which looked like a black splinter. The sac had been broken, allowing the poison to enter the child's arm. No wonder she was in pain!

'Come on Abigail, stand up,' urged her mother kindly.

Abigail started to sit up and then collapsed backwards. Trudi noticed with concern that the child's face had gone very pale and that she was having difficulty in breathing.

'Abigail,' said Trudi, 'can you hear me? Can you say, "Yes"?'

The child didn't reply but seemed to be slipping into unconsciousness. Trudi felt her pulse. It was racing.

'Oh, good heavens,' said Trudi under her breath. 'I think we may have to get your daughter to hospital,' she told the mother. 'It looks as though she may have suffered an anaphylactic attack.'

The mother looked puzzled and alarmed in equal measure. 'A what?'

'Abigail seems to have suffered a severe allergic reaction to the sting. She had a bee sting once before, you said, and that may have sensitised her body to them. We must act quickly. It can be very dangerous.' Trudi could have said 'life-threatening' but hadn't wanted to cause the mother to panic.

She stood up and waved her arms around and shouted, 'Dan! Dan! Come quickly!'

Then she bent down to the almost limp body of the child and put her on her side in the recovery position to help her breathing, which was now very shallow and intermittent.

Dan, on seeing and hearing Trudi's alarm signal, left the two boys in the care of a couple of women who were minding their own children and dashed across the grass to the bench where Trudi had been sitting. He could see a small child lying on the grass.

'It's anaphylactic shock—bee sting,' Trudi told him succinctly.

By giving the child a very quick examination, Dan could tell that Trudi's diagnosis was correct. There was no time to lose. The child was still breathing, but only just. Her air passages had swelled and virtually closed and her pulse was so fast it felt like machine-gun fire.

'Where's my bag?' he asked. Trudi, who'd anticipated his request, handed it to him.

'Hope you've got some adrenalin in there,' she said.

'Never without it,' said Dan, who hoped he was right.

He found the vial and disinfected the rubber stopper with an alcohol swab. After calculating the dosage, he drew the clear liquid into a disposable syringe. He checked it for air bubbles then removed the needle from the vial. Trudi, in the meantime, had prepared an area for the injection on the child's unswollen right upper arm by cleansing the site with an antiseptic wipe.

Dan pinched a small area of the cleansed site, inserted the needle and slowly injected the adrenalin. Trudi massaged the site for a few seconds while Dan replaced the needle in its special container for disposal.

The child's recovery was almost instantaneous, her breathing quickly returning to normal as the colour flooded back into her face.

By this time Abigail's mother was in a state of shock and sat down heavily on the park bench.

'Is she going to be all right?' she asked, her voice tense and fearful.

'Yes,' Dan reassured her. 'She'll be fine, but I'd like her to go to hospital for a good check-over. I'll phone for an ambulance on my mobile.'

'You were fantastic,' said the mother, breathing a deep sigh of relief. 'Both of you. Are you in the St John Ambulance or something?'

Trudi smiled. 'Dan's a doctor and I'm a nurse.'

Abigail was now sitting on her mother's knee, being cuddled and comforted. Trudi was phoning for an ambulance.

It arrived within ten minutes and Abigail and her mother and little brother were led safely inside by the paramedics to whom Dan explained the situation.

'Thank you again,' said the woman to Trudi. 'Both you and your husband were wonderful. I don't know what we'd have done without you.'

As they walked back to collect the four children, who were being minded by various concerned adults, Dan gave Trudi a sly look.

'You and your husband, eh?'

'It was a conclusion she jumped to,' explained Trudi, blushing. 'It wasn't anything I'd said.'

'It's quite a nice conclusion to jump to, though, isn't it?' mused Dan. 'I quite like the idea of people thinking we're a married couple with all these kids. It rather appeals to me.'

Although he spoke in a jesting fashion, it gave Trudi a warm glow. Yes, she also liked the idea of people thinking they were a married couple with lots of children. Dream on, Trudi, dream on.

Back at the house later on, Trudi and Dan prepared lunch for the children.

Clare had left copious notes covering every aspect of the children's routine—meals and rest times, where to find every conceivable item of children's clothing, bedding and, of course, ample supplies of disposable nappies.

The three youngest children had naps after lunch, but Liam at three and a half announced that he was 'too big to go to sleep in the afternoon'.

'Pity,' said Dan under his breath but loud enough for Trudi to hear. 'I was hoping for a bit of a lie-down myself.' He gave her a look which sent tingles up her spine.

Liam was in his element. He now had the full attention of two adults while the little ones where taking their 'baby naps'. He made the most of it, demanding full participation in all his games.

First of all he was a bus driver, with Trudi and Dan as the passengers. He made them wait at an imaginary bus stop, then sit on the stairs which doubled as his imaginary bus.

'You haven't paid your fares!' he said, insisting that they get up and hand him the money before being allowed back to their seats.

Then he wanted help with constructing a very ambitious Lego project. And finally, when Trudi and Dan were nearly dropping with exhaustion, Liam invented another game called 'Farmer', which involved him driving round the house on his toy tractor and ordering them to do all the work.

'I spot a young man with great management potential,' said Dan, sinking down in an armchair after he'd decided that enough was enough. 'I'm withdrawing my labour, Liam. And so is Trudi. We're going on strike.'

'What's that?' asked their small tormentor. 'What's "strike"?'

'You'll learn soon enough, young man, if you treat your employees the way you've been treating us for the past two hours!' Dan yawned and was about to close his eyes for a brief moment when a little voice called from upstairs.

'Can we get up now?' It was Callum.

Trudi looked across at Dan and couldn't help laughing. 'And you were the one who liked the idea of having lots of children! It's pretty hard work, isn't it?'

'You're telling me! Give me a double single-handed paediatric cardiac clinic followed by a double cardiology teaching session any day!'

By the time all four children had been played with all afternoon, given their tea and baths and had had bedtime stories read to them or songs sung, Dan and Trudi were totally exhausted.

Trudi had agreed to stay the night. There was a spare cot for Grace and as all the children were getting on so well it seemed a shame to leave. She *did* wonder how Dan would have coped on his own if she'd gone—particularly if there'd been a problem with one of the children during the night. He was an excellent paediatrician, but as a childless bachelor he could well have been out of his depth, trying to manage the three children on his own. In fact, she was amazed that Clare and Jim had even considered it. Trudi didn't know for sure, but she suspected that getting her to stay overnight with Dan was all part of Clare's plan to throw the two of them together. She'd even left a casserole and a bottle of wine for their evening meal, with a note saying, 'To be eaten by candlelight!'

Dan cradled his wineglass and leaned back in his chair with a contented sigh.

'That was a superb meal. One of the best chicken casseroles I've ever tasted.'

'It was pork, I think,' corrected Trudi. 'But, whatever it was, it tasted great. Actually, we were both so tired and hungry we'd have eaten a horse!'

Dan gazed at Trudi across the candle flame.

'You know, you look marvellous when you're knackered.'

'Thanks a lot! And here was I thinking that my quick wash and brush-up after putting the kids to bed had transformed me!'

Dan's eyes softened as he took in her sexily drowsy appearance—the hastily brushed hair and slightly smudged eye make-up. As she stifled a yawn he stretched out a hand and touched hers.

'I love you just the way you are. Don't change a thing for me.'

Entwining his long fingers round hers, he stood up and pulled her gently towards him.

'I want you in my arms.'

He kissed her, a warm, loving, tender kiss that set her heart pounding and made her tired body go weak. She leaned against him, supported only by the strength of his arms.

'Is this really happening to us?' he murmured huskily.

'I was going to ask you the same question,' she replied breathlessly, 'because I've never felt this way before. You're so special, Dan…'

He kissed her again, this time more hungrily, as if swept along by a tide of mounting passion.

She put a hand to his cheek and stroked the hard angles of it, loving the faint prickling of his stubbled skin against her own.

'I want you,' she whispered, unable to fight her feelings any longer.

'Oh, my darling,' he said huskily, holding her to him, making her feel safe and secure. 'How I've longed to hear you say that. I thought you might still be thinking of that other man…'

'Don't ever think that,' she replied softly in his ear. 'There are things in my past but—'

'I don't want to know. If it makes you unhappy to tell me, then I don't want to know.'

Was it the wine, or her tiredness, or the magic of the evening? For suddenly all Trudi's problems seemed far away. The only reality was that she was in Dan's arms where she'd longed to be…and that he demanded no explanations about her past or about the father of her child.

The emotion and the relief were almost overwhelming. Her eyes brimmed.

'You're crying,' said Dan, kissing the tears from her lashes. Then, with a swift movement of his hand, he extinguished the candle flame. He led her by the hand and they walked like two shadows up the stairs and into the bedroom.

He took his clothes off quickly and then slowly undressed her until they stood naked together in the moonlight.

The fire of passion now licked through them both and their bodies, previously tired and exhausted, sprang to life. He devoured her with his lips and his hands, covering her body with his warm sensual touch. Lifting her gently onto the bed, he caressed her again with his lips until she moaned in pleasure. A hand cupped one of her breasts, the sensitive flesh of her nipple responding instantly to the sweet sensation of his touch as he stroked it insistently with his thumb. Then he took each aroused nipple in his mouth and gently ran his tongue over the hard peaks until she wanted to cry out loud with the exquisite torment. His breathing quickened as his body pressed against hers and she arched towards him.

They clung to each other in throbbing rapture, desire hitting them with the force of a tidal wave.

'Let me love you now,' said Dan urgently, his voice thick and husky.

'But what about…?' Even through her mounting

desire for him, a small practical voice spoke in the back of her head. 'I'm not on the Pill,' she said haltingly, for a moment bringing them down to reality.

'What? Oh, yes, I see.' He pulled back reluctantly. 'You don't want another baby yet, is that it?'

'I'd love another baby. I just don't want to have one by accident, that's all.'

'You think I'll desert you if you get pregnant, is that it? You think you'll be left on your own like you were with Grace?'

Before he'd got the words out he regretted them. He'd promised himself he wouldn't bring up her past and here he was, doing just that.

She tensed and rolled away from him.

'I'm sorry, Trudi. I didn't mean to say that. I just wanted you to know that it will be different for us. I want to marry you. I want us to be a real family, like we were today. Have lots of kids. All that kind of thing. And if you get pregnant tonight, that's fine with me.'

Trudi responded by turning to him again. She had to stop being so sensitive whenever he mentioned her past. Dan was a good man and had made it clear he loved her and wasn't after a one-night stand. But was she ready to risk getting pregnant so soon…so soon into their relationship? And so soon after having Grace? After all, she wasn't even a year old. How much better it would be if she and Dan could just enjoy a loving relationship without the added complication of pregnancy. There'd be plenty of time for babies after they were married.

Married! It had only just sunk in. Dan had said he wanted to marry her!

She snuggled up to him, running her hands over his broad chest. 'I want us to have a family soon...but not just yet,' she said huskily.

'In that case, you'd better stop doing that!' He moved her hand which had strayed sensually downwards, following the line of his hip bone. 'At least until I pay a visit to the chemist tomorrow.'

They slipped under the duvet and fell asleep in each other's arms.

CHAPTER EIGHT

'I REALLY like it in Orthopaedics,' said Shelly when Trudi bumped into her several weeks after the accident.

Her former nurse had now settled back into work—but in a different department, much to Trudi's relief.

'I'm very glad they offered me this job on the children's ward.' Shelly looked a new person, new and improved. 'Now I get the chance to do some *real* nursing,' she continued. 'I don't even mind doing the night shifts. It's all very rewarding. But I suppose that's what nursing's all about—a vocation, isn't it?'

Trudi bit her lip. Who was this paragon standing before her? Could this be the same self-centred Shelly who'd made her working life a misery when she'd been in her department? She could only assume that the accident had produced a lasting effect and that the young nurse had truly learned her lesson.

'And isn't it good news about Kev?' she gushed. It was obvious that the accident still preyed on her mind...as well it might.

'Marvellous news,' agreed Trudi. 'When I phoned last week they said he would probably be going home in a day or so.'

'I spoke to Karen yesterday and she said he's coming out today!'

'That is great news,' responded Trudi. Karen was

still not back at work. She had suffered quite badly from post-accident trauma and was still undergoing counselling.

'So, how's things with you down at Outpatients?'

'Same as usual…busy as usual…lots of patients as usual.'

'I meant you personally. You look…different.' Shelly cast a critical eye over Trudi. She couldn't quite put her finger on it, but her former staff sister was looking…*prettier*. She said it out loud. 'You look prettier.'

Trudi was staggered that Shelly should even notice how she looked and was so taken aback that she found herself blushing.

'Nice of you to say so, Shelly. It's probably because my daughter's growing up and isn't quite so demanding. She had her first birthday last week.' Trudi was about to launch into a description of Grace's party when she realised that there was a limit to the 'new' Shelly, and that hearing details about Grace was probably pushing it a bit. She glanced at her watch.

'Clinic starts soon. See you again, Shelly… Oh, and good luck.'

The two nurses were about to walk in opposite directions when Shelly touched Trudi's arm for a second, as if struck by an afterthought.

'By the way,' she said, 'I found out why that louse Simon wanted me to say I'd been driving his car that night.'

'Apart from the fact he was drunk, you mean?'

'Yes. He'd been previously disqualified, so that

was another thing they've got him for—driving while disqualified.'

Trudi shook her head. 'Louse,' she repeated. She didn't add, Well, I did warn you. She felt that Shelly had suffered enough for her mistake.

'Well, see you,' said Shelly.

'Yes. See you.'

As she walked back to Outpatients, Trudi looked at her reflection in the windows and glass doors as she passed.

I suppose I do look different, she mused to herself. That's what love can do.

She and Dan were now an item. They made an effort to keep it a secret from their work colleagues, purely to give themselves more privacy. One thing they each hated was the idea of being talked about and their affair being discussed openly in the hospital. But it wasn't a mega-secret. Clare and Jim knew about it, for instance. And Trudi had confided in Stella and Joan, the two agency nurses who were now working on a regular contract in her department. She knew they weren't gossipy types and she appreciated their common-sense attitude and advice.

'He seems a really nice man,' said Stella. 'I've heard nothing but good of him in the hospital. He's great with his little patients and a model consultant to work with.'

'Really nice but also very sexy,' said Joan with a wink. 'That's the best combination! You don't want the type who's some sort of flighty gigolo who'll be having affairs left, right and centre, do you?'

It made Trudi smile to hear these two middle-aged women talking with authority about Dan, whom they only knew from the weekly clinics. But it was nice to get such general approval of her man.

Her man! The words made Trudi feel all funny inside. And when she tested the words 'my husband' to herself—as she did several times a day—it made her whole being glow with happiness. Maybe that's what Shelly had picked up on. Since her relationship with Dan had taken off she was truly a different person. All her anxieties and concerns from the past seemed to have vanished. They were still there, of course, lying quietly below the surface. But in time, once she was married to Dan, her worries would be buried so deep she would never have to think about them again!

It was all so simple. Because Dan had insisted he wasn't interested in knowing about her past—and the man who was Grace's father—Trudi would never have to reveal the surrogacy. There was no way he was going to find out unless she told him…and she would never do that. It was her own business and Dan need never know about it. Why rake up problems from the past when they had their whole future to look forward to? And she *was* looking forward to it…longing for it. Everything…living together, sharing their lives…their children. He would make a marvellous father, she predicted. He was so wonderful with Grace and he treated her as if she were his own child.

'A child needs a father,' he said one day when he was letting Grace climb all over him as he lay on the floor. 'If only to use as a climbing frame.'

At Grace's first birthday party, he'd insisted on being the host, welcoming the little ones, playing games with them and dishing out the jelly and cake like an old hand.

'I like this fatherhood lark,' he'd said, as Trudi had wiped a smear of chocolate pudding from his nose.

One of the benefits of letting Clare and Jim in on their romance was that Clare was extremely willing to have Grace for the day while Dan and Trudi went sailing. Dan, who'd joined the local sailing club at Windmill Mere, was a very keen sailor. For years he'd kept a small sailing dinghy which he took out whenever he got the opportunity. Trudi had never sailed before but he encouraged her to come along and crew for him.

'It's dead easy,' he said. 'All you do is sit at the front and do what I tell you.'

'What will I wear?'

'I've got spare waterproofs and life jacket, so just come as you are. Bring a spare set of clothes in case we capsize.'

'Capsize?' gulped Trudi nervously.

'That's all part of the fun,' joked Dan. 'We sail on a very safe, small lake, with a rescue boat always in attendance on race days. So, if we go over, we get rescued and then get a free cup of tea.'

'I'm sorry? Did you say free cup of tea?'

'I can see I'm going too fast for you.' Dan laughed. 'It's an old custom. When you get back to the clubhouse you get a free cup of tea if you've capsized. Some people do it just for that!'

He made it all sound such fun. And it was.

The first time he took her there they just pottered

about the lake while Dan explained the simple ru-
diments of dinghy sailing.

'As long as you remember to duck whenever the
boom is about to swing across, you'll be fine. I'll
shout ''Ready about'' just to warn you.'

It was a glorious day, the sun reflecting off the
water and the birds singing their hearts out. A gentle
breeze was blowing, just enough for Dan and Trudi
to practise sailing manoeuvres—but not so strong as
to put them in any danger of capsizing.

'With a bit of practice you'll be able to lean out
over the side like I'm doing now,' he said, leaning
out over the water whenever a small gust of wind
threatened to unbalance the boat.

Trudi, who loved the outdoor life, was beginning
to get the hang of things and really started to enjoy
herself. She had complete faith in Dan as they sailed
up and down the lake. She even enjoyed the times
when the wind dropped completely and they were
left in idleness. At those times Dan would slide into
the seat next to her and talk about all sorts of
things—how he, too, loved the open-air life, and how
as a young boy he'd loved spending time with an
uncle who'd lived in a farm cottage in the Yorkshire
Dales.

'He lived in a village called Chrishallthwaite in
Swaledale, in a valley where two rivers meet. On a
summer's day it's heaven on earth and in the winter,
when the snow lies deep, it's a magical place.'

'Tell me about it,' she prompted. Her eyes glis-
tened as he went on to tell her more about the little
Yorkshire village that he remembered as his idyll.

'I'd love to go there,' she breathed. 'It sounds like

a place where you could lose all your troubles…an ideal hide-away.'

'It is. I often go there in my dreams. Does that sound silly?'

'Not at all. So your uncle was a farmer?'

'No such luck,' said Dan. 'He was a farm labourer and shepherd. He had this little tied cottage that came with the job and I thought it was the most wonderful place in the world. It had a brook nearby and soft, rolling hills all around. You could see lambs gambolling on the hillside outside the back door. He was up from dawn till dusk…tending the sheep, repairing the walls, working in the fields.'

As he spoke of his early life, Dan's Yorkshire accent became more pronounced. Trudi loved it. She thought it suited him perfectly. She loved the earthy resonance his voice took on whenever he became a 'real Yorkshireman', dropping the slightly more polished tones he'd acquired over the years.

Dan kept his hand steady on the tiller as a small gust of wind moved the boat.

Trudi studied his face in profile as he stared out across the lake. She loved him so desperately…and knowing that he'd worked so hard, coming from such a poor family, it made her love him even more. Their relationship was turning into the most satisfying experience of her life.

They'd made love the previous night, all night, with ecstatic fulfilment, his body taking hers to heights of sexual pleasure she hadn't believed possible. In the early hours of the morning she'd felt, once more, the stirring rise of his flesh and her own breathing quickening in response. 'You're insatiable,' she'd said, laughing but loving the delicious way her insides had started to melt as he'd begun moving against her. Afterwards, when she'd lain naked and exhausted in his arms, she hadn't been able to imagine feeling happier or more contented.

'I think you've probably had enough for one day,' said Dan, heading the boat towards the landing stage. 'I don't want to overdo it the first time and put you off for good.'

'You won't do that,' said Trudi with slight disappointment. She'd imagined they would be sailing for a least a couple more hours.

'I have other plans for us,' he said.

'Oh, I see,' said Trudi with a smile, thinking he was referring to bed.

'I don't think you do,' he said. 'I've made some appointments for this afternoon.'

Seeing the disappointment on her face, he laughed. 'Not work-type appointments! Appointments with an estate agent.'

'Estate agent?'

'He's looking for suitable houses and cottages for us.'

Trudi's heart gave a leap. 'For us?'

'Of course, "for us", you silly woman! You don't think I'm going to buy a house for myself, do you? We're getting married. And we can't possibly all live in that tiny place of yours. I like space to spread out—and to have somewhere to keep my boat in the winter.'

She looked at him under her eyelashes. She hadn't thought that far ahead, but how wonderful to be going house-hunting with him. Had she really thought they would live in her small terraced house? Trudi had got so used to the idea of providing for herself and Grace for the foreseeable future that she hadn't yet adjusted to the fact that being married to Dan would mean rethinking her whole lifestyle.

'You've got some houses to look at?'

'*We* have. I'm not going to buy anything unless you're happy with it. There were two houses that caught my eye from the estate agent's details. They're both large detached properties with big gardens—in the country but close enough to town so that I'm not spending hours travelling each day.'

'That's important for me, too. I don't fancy spending hours travelling either—it would cut down the time I have to spend with Grace.'

He leaned across the boat and touched her hand. 'Sweetheart, once we're married it will be *your* choice whether or not you go back to work. I know how much you hate leaving Grace. If you want to stay at home, that's all right with me. It will be your decision. Money doesn't enter into it. We can well afford for you not to work, if that's what you want.'

Trudi blinked back a tear. *How* she'd wished for the past year that she'd been able to stay at home and look after Grace full time. When her daughter went to school then she might want to do a part-time job, like Clare had. For Trudi, that would be the ideal situation…and now it was coming true!

'In a minute I want you to get ready to jump off the boat as I bring it in. Take the painter with you—that rope at the front—and pull it through one of the metal rings on the jetty.'

Dan let the sails flap to slow down their approach.

Trudi waited until he'd brought the dinghy alongside the wooden landing stage jutting out into the lake and then jumped onto it with one brave leap…as instructed. Then she pulled the painter through one of the jetty rings. Dan was impressed.

'We're going to make a brilliant sailor out of you! I even think we might try some racing next week.'

'I don't know if I'm quite up to that,' replied Trudi nervously.

'Nonsense,' he replied. 'You're a good deal better than many others who crew here, believe me. So we'll come racing next week—and afterwards there's a jazz evening which is always very popular, I've been told. A band called the Swamptown Stompers are playing.'

'I'd love to come. I think I've heard of the Swamptown Stompers,' she mused, 'but I can't remember where or when. It's a name that rings a bell somehow.'

They had a quick lunch at the sailing club, then set off to keep the first house-viewing appointment.

Dan had handed her the estate agent's details for the two houses they were going to be looking at. Trudi was as impressed by the photographs and descriptions as she was staggered by the prices.

'They're so expensive!' she gasped. 'I had no idea house prices had shot up so much.'

'They're in a ''very desirable and sought-after area''—as estate-agent-speak has it. I've waited long enough to buy a house, Trudi, and I'm going to make sure it's the biggest and nicest I can afford.'

'Do we really need such a big house?'

Dan slammed down into low gear as they climbed up a steep hill that ran through a wooded landscape.

'Put it down to my upbringing,' he said.

'Upbringing? You told me that your parents brought you up in a tiny house!'

'Precisely.'

Following the estate agent's instructions, they found the first house without much difficulty. It was big all right. Far too big, decided Trudi. Dan wasn't so keen either.

'It didn't feel like a home.' That was the only comment he made.

The second house, three miles away, was a completely different proposition. It was more compact and had a glorious south-facing garden. There was a low swing with a little girl playing on it. Trudi imagined the scene in two or three years' time when Grace could be doing the same.

The house was perfect…not too big, not too small.

Dan slipped an arm round her as they stared out of a bedroom window across the well-manicured lawns.

'I think this is it, don't you?'

'Yes.' She hugged Dan impetuously. 'Yes, please!'

'Do you want a big wedding or a small one?'

Dan's question, as they drove away from the second house, took her by surprise.

'Wedding? Oh, yes, I'd forgotten about that. I mean, I know we're getting married—I just hadn't given it too much thought. You hadn't mentioned it before, that's all.'

'I wanted us to find a house first, that's why. I'm

an old-fashioned guy and want to do things in the right order—you know, find the girl, find the house, organise the wedding, get the ring.'

Trudi laughed at the way he reeled it off. 'I'd quite like a small wedding if it's all the same with you. As it is, it will be mainly your family coming, not mine.'

Dan covered her hand with his. 'We can make it very small, if you want. Just us and Clare and Jim as witnesses. How does that sound?'

'Sounds just perfect.'

'In that case, we'll set the date to tie in with the house purchase…which should be in about six weeks' time, according to the estate agent. And you can give your notice at the hospital whenever it suits you. Now, where shall we go on honeymoon?'

It was all too much for Trudi. She pretended to collapse down in her car seat. 'You're a fast worker, Dan Donovan! Give a girl chance to get her breath!'

'Not likely. I'm going to catch you while I can, before you change your mind.' He pulled the car off the country road and into a lay-by, and switched off the engine. Releasing the seat belts, he pulled her to him and kissed her hungrily. He glanced briefly at his watch.

'If I take you home now, we've still got an hour or so before Clare brings Grace back to you, haven't we?'

She nodded in confirmation. He started the engine and headed towards her village.

The delicious flame of desire began to rise in her body…for although they drove in silence she knew exactly what he had in mind for when they got home.

*   *   *

The following Saturday, Dan took her sailing again as arranged and this time they joined in the club races. She saw a completely different side of the man she was going to marry.

'There's a ruthless streak in you, Dan Donovan!' she shouted over the noise of the flapping sails as they jostled for position with other boats.

'Shocks you, does it?'

'No, it amuses me. If they could see you back at the hospital now! They'd soon change their minds about your image as "the gentleman cardiologist", I can tell you!'

'Listen, it's important to get round the marker buoys ahead of the crowd or you lose position in the race!'

Trudi grinned. She liked seeing him like this…completely absorbed in his sailing almost to the exclusion of everything else. When he worked so hard at the hospital and, in his own words, was in danger of becoming a workaholic, it was good that he could detach himself and lose himself in something else.

'I quite like you being masterful,' she said jokingly. 'Just as long as you confine all this ordering me about to the sailing club.'

Her words drifted over him as he was concentrating hard on rounding the next buoy.

'Ready about!' He pushed the tiller across and the boom swung round as the sails filled with wind, taking them past several other boats in the race. A look of triumph crossed his face.

'Just look how much we've gained on the field!

Now, what was that you were saying before we rounded the buoy?'

'Nothing.' She laughed. 'Nothing of any importance.'

It was the day of the jazz evening and Dan and Trudi had brought the clothes that they'd be wearing with them to save an extra car journey.

They showered in the clubhouse and changed ready for the evening's entertainment. It wasn't a 'posh do', Dan had told her, so she wore her best pair of chinos and a silk jersey blouse in peach, which went perfectly with the auburn tones of her straight-cut, chin-length hair.

There was a barbecue to start off the evening. Trudi and Dan lined up with dozens of other sailing-club members and their guests on the lawn outside the clubhouse amid the mouth-watering aromas, where the sizzling food that had been cooked over hot coals was being served.

They joined a group of people and were thoroughly enjoying themselves. Dan introduced her to everyone as his fiancée. After the first time, he whispered in her ear, 'With all this house-buying I've forgotten to get you an engagement ring!'

Trudi waved a chicken leg breezily in the air. 'We're getting married in six weeks' time so it's hardly worth spending the money on an engagement ring. But thanks for the offer!'

Midway through the food, the jazz band arrived and started setting up their equipment in the large bar area of the clubhouse.

'The Swamptown Stompers are great!' said a woman next to Trudi, whose name she couldn't recall—there'd been so many introductions she had no hope of remembering them all.

'So I've heard,' she replied, meaning that Dan had told her. But at the back of her mind was a niggling question—where else had she heard about them before?

'They play New Orleans jazz,' said the woman.

'That's my favourite kind,' replied Trudi.

'Then you're in for a treat tonight.'

As the band started up, the music drew the people inside like a magnet. Dan took Trudi by the hand and led her through the now-crowded room to the small dance floor where people of all ages, shapes and sizes were dancing away to the compulsive, foot-tapping rhythm.

After a couple of rousing numbers, the band played Trudi's favourite…'Georgia'. She and Dan clung to each other, her body pressed close to his as they moved in harmony to the slow, sensual beat. Trudi had shut her eyes, leaning her head on Dan's shoulder. Then something made her open them…a feeling that she was being watched.

Across the room she glimpsed a familiar face… and a familiar pair of eyes boring into her. She went rigid with shock. Standing next to the band, holding a glass of beer, was her former best friend and colleague from Mayside General…Annie.

Now she remembered where she'd heard of the Swamptown Stompers! Annie's boyfriend was one of the musicians in the band. She didn't recall what he played—only that Annie had always gone on about how great they were and what a terrific musician her boyfriend was.

As Dan and Trudi moved around the dance floor she realised with horror that they were getting closer and closer to Annie, who was staring at them—and in particular at Trudi—as if she'd seen a ghost.

'What's the matter?' asked Dan. 'You've gone all stiff and unresponsive. Did I step on your foot?'

'No, you didn't.'

'Then I must have lost the knack of dancing with you. Perhaps you're tired after all that sailing today. Do you want to sit down?'

'Yes. Please.'

Trudi could hardly speak she was so tense. As they pushed their way back across the crowded dance floor she saw out of the corner of her eye that Annie had put down the glass of beer and was trying to follow them.

Panic rose in her throat.

'I'll see you in a minute, Dan. I've just got to speak to someone I've just seen. Won't be long.'

She separated from him and went outside into the fresh air. Annie followed her.

'Trudi! It's you, isn't it?' she said, throwing her arms around her former friend.

'Annie!' she said, her eyes blurring with tears.

'Where on earth have you been?' said Annie. 'I tried for ages to get in touch with you but the trail just seemed to go dead.'

'I had to go away... I just had to. But I've missed you so much!' She clung to Annie, hugging her old friend fiercely.

'So what happened? Where did you go?' asked Annie after a few moments. 'No one knew where you were. You left no forwarding address and...'

Annie threw her hands in the air in a gesture of desperation. 'I've been so *worried* about you!'

'I'm fine,' Trudi reassured her, perilously close to bursting into tears. 'I felt bad about not telling you where I was, but things worked out very differently from how I'd imagined they would and…'

'If you felt bad, how do you think I felt?' said Annie, biting her lip, remembering the last time they'd spoken and the unfeeling things she'd said to her friend.

'You were my best friend,' she continued, 'and then we had that terrible row about the surrogacy and everything. I wanted to tell you how sorry I was that I said all those hurtful things… but I couldn't find you. I thought that maybe you'd done something, you know, reckless…'

Trudi put an arm round Annie and walked her a little further away from the clubhouse and into the shadows. The last thing she wanted was for Dan to overhear this particular conversation!

'I never found out what happened to you…about the baby.' Annie's face was a picture of misery. 'I should have been there to give you support, to help you, to be there for you in your hour of need. And what did I do? Just said horrid insensitive things…'

'It's all right now, Annie,' Trudi said. 'I've got a nice job and a nice little house and everything's great.'

'What about the baby? Did you give it to your sister?'

'My sister died.'

'Oh, my God!' Annie put her hand to her face on hearing this shocking news.

'I kept the baby. She's mine. You said I'd never be able to give her up, and in a way you were right. But, of course, I never had the chance to find out.'

It was now Annie's turn to put a comforting hand on her friend's shoulder.

'Oh, you poor girl. What a terrible time you've had…and I feel awful because I wasn't around to help you through it. Trudi, I'm sorry—for *everything*!'

'That's all in the past now, Annie. I've got a new life and a new man…'

She could have bitten off her own tongue. What was she thinking of, telling Annie about Dan? Her new life with him depended on her never revealing details of her past life and the surrogate pregnancy. All the colour drained from her face.

'You mean that dishy man I saw you dancing with? Is he the new man in your life?'

'Er, yes…' Trudi hesitated. 'Look, here's my address…' She scribbled it down for Annie. 'Come round and see me, and the baby, soon.'

She didn't go straight back into the clubhouse with Annie, making an excuse that she needed to get something from the car. What she needed was time to think. The evening had turned out to be quite traumatic for her. She was delighted to meet up with Annie again, but it had brought its own problems with it. It meant she was getting nearer to the time when she had to tell Dan the whole truth. In her heart she knew she would have to face up to it some time or other…but tonight? What if Annie came over to join them and mentioned it? Perhaps she should have sworn her to secrecy, but she just hadn't been thinking straight at that precise moment.

Trudi started to panic. She didn't know what her plan of action was going to be, only that she had to get out of there…quickly.

Instead of going back into the clubhouse, Trudi slipped around the side of the building and ran up the path to the road. She hadn't brought a handbag with her that day, just a small bag that attached to her belt and contained credit cards, a little money and her house keys.

The top road led to a major road. She didn't stop running until she reached it and stood under one of the highway lighting pylons, catching her breath. There was very little traffic and she was desperately wondering what to do next when she spied a minicab driving along with its sign lit up.

She flagged it down.

The driver rolled down the window. 'I'm not supposed to pick up fares unless they're prebooked,' he said, looking her up and down, trying to judge whether he was being set up for a prosecution.

Regardless, Trudi got in the back seat.

'I'm not going to report you if that's what's worrying you. I just need to get home pretty damn quickly. I live ten miles in that direction.' In her present state her voice had taken on a commanding tone which implied that she was a woman not to be messed with.

'Righty-ho, lady. You're the boss!'

She fell back in the seat with relief and nervous exhaustion.

What was she doing? She'd run away from Annie

and Dan…and had persuaded a poor taxi driver to break the law, and all because of what? All because she couldn't face the truth—that Dan was now going to find out the kind of person she really was. Why *hadn't* she sworn Annie to secrecy? 'Damn,' she muttered under her breath. But even as the idea crossed her mind she knew it would never have worked in the long term. She *had* to tell Dan…but right now she needed space for herself, space to get her thoughts in order and work out how, and when, she was going to tell him.

CHAPTER NINE

Dan had queued at the bar for several minutes, buying drinks for himself and Trudi. When he'd got them and had pushed his way through the crowded room with the glasses, carefully avoiding spilling their contents over himself or on the floor, he looked around for her.

Where was she? He peered outside and couldn't see her among the people still lining up at the barbecue for food. Perhaps she'd gone to the Ladies?

He sat on one of the benches on the veranda outside the clubhouse and, putting her glass carefully on the floor next to the bench, took a few swigs from his cool beer. He was a happy, contented man. His emotional life had taken an upward path and was now, at last, catching up with his professional life. He found himself smiling for no apparent reason. He had so much to look forward to—a satisfying medical career, a glorious house that he'd just agreed to buy. But, better than any of that, at last he'd found a girl with whom he wanted to spend the rest of his life.

But where was she? It was now twenty minutes since she'd left him on the dance floor, saying she wanted to speak to someone, and had walked out of the clubhouse with a dark-haired girl. He'd looked all around and couldn't find her...and if she'd subsequently gone to the Ladies, surely she would have been back by now?

He finished his beer and, holding her drink, walked back into the noisy room. He could see the dark-haired girl Trudi had been speaking to…but she was now alone, standing by the side of the band. He went over to her during a pause in the music.

'I'm looking for someone called Trudi,' he said to the girl. 'Wasn't she with you about half an hour ago?'

'Yes, she was,' answered Annie. 'But I don't know where she is now. I was wondering myself where she was.'

Dan returned to the bar and put Trudi's drink down on it. He sat on a high bar stool facing the dance floor. He spent several more minutes scouring the crowd for a glimpse of her. After another twenty minutes he went back and spoke again to the dark-haired girl.

'Do you think that Trudi might be in the Ladies?' he asked. 'Would you have a quick look in there for me? Perhaps she's not feeling well.'

'Sure,' said Annie, equally puzzled by Trudi's apparent disappearance.

A few minutes later she returned, shrugging her shoulders. 'She's not there. There's nobody in there at all.'

'Then where is she?' For the first time a suspicion entered his mind that something might be wrong… that Trudi had gone missing.

The jazz band had started up again and Dan could hardly make himself heard over the music. He took

Annie by the arm and walked her out of the noisy clubhouse onto the veranda steps.

'Tell me what happened when you two were talking out here.'

'It was about old times, really. I said I was sorry and everything…' She trailed off as memories of the conversation caught up with her.

'What about old times?' persisted Dan. 'What kind of things?'

He was beginning to realise that he knew very little about Trudi and her friends from the past. Every time he broached the subject she clammed up or flew off the handle. In the end he'd given up trying to find out what had happened to make her so touchy whenever the subject was raised. He loved her for what she was and didn't care about any of that. But now that she seemed to have disappeared he needed to probe to get a clue to her odd behaviour—and to find out if she was perhaps in any danger.

'What kind of things?' he repeated when Annie remained silent.

'About why she left Mayside General in such a hurry,' explained Annie. 'And we hugged each other and she gave me her new address and we agreed to keep in touch…because we were best friends at one time.'

'Did she say where she was going when you'd finished talking?' Dan was becoming increasingly concerned.

'She said she had to get something from the car, I think.'

'How strange,' said Dan. 'She hasn't got a set of my car keys.'

'Maybe she went home with someone else?' ventured Annie, adding hastily, 'Not that I want to hint at anything… Was there any disagreement between the two of you?'

Dan breathed out in frustration. 'No.'

Why should Trudi disappear? *Had* she gone home? He took out his mobile phone and called her number. It rang for ages but there was no answer.

There was nothing for it but to drive to her house and see if she was there. How she could have got home was a mystery, but he was running out of ideas. Before leaving, he wrote a message for Trudi and handed it to one of the bar staff. He described her to them and asked if they could keep an eye out for her in case she turned up after he'd left.

He drove the ten miles to her village, filled with foreboding. He'd never had an experience like this before…when someone just disappeared for no apparent reason. He put the possibility of a crime to the back of his mind. It wasn't something he could grapple with right now…

When he reached her house it was in darkness. It looked the same as when he'd picked her up that morning—and even though it was now dark, the curtains hadn't been drawn. He peered through the windows but could see no sign of life. Then a shiver ran through him as he turned to face the road. Trudi's car was missing! It had been parked outside her house this morning in the spot where his own car now stood.

An explanation occurred to him.

'Of course! She's gone to pick up the baby from my sister's!'

They'd taken Grace to Clare's for the day while they'd gone sailing and on to the jazz evening. But he'd been under the impression that Grace was going to stay the night at his sister's and that Trudi would pick her up in the morning.

Attempting to make the pieces of jigsaw fit, Dan jumped into his car and headed off to his sister's house.

Ringing the doorbell and banging on the door at the same time, he realised what a state of panic he'd got himself into.

A bleary-eyed Clare in her nightdress opened the door.

'Hush, you'll wake the whole house, if you haven't already!' She stepped aside to let him in.

'I'm looking for Trudi,' he blurted out.

'What's going on between you two?' she asked with a yawn.

'What do you mean?'

'She was here an hour ago to pick up Grace and said that I was to tell you she'd gone away for a few days and that you weren't to worry about her.'

Dan was stunned.

'Gone away? What do you mean, gone away? Where has she gone? And why?'

'This is like the Spanish Inquisition,' said Clare, giving another big yawn. 'She didn't say where and she didn't say why. Have you two fallen out over something?'

'No,' said Dan, 'at least I don't think we have. I'm not too sure about anything any more.'

'If you two have quarrelled then I think you should

go and make it up. You're getting married in a few weeks, remember.'

'We haven't had a quarrel and, yes, I do remember that we're getting married in a few weeks' time,' snapped Dan.

'Don't take it out on me,' responded Clare. 'Don't shoot the messenger just because you don't like the message!'

'I'm sorry,' said Dan. Then he had a cheering thought. 'Maybe she hasn't set off yet. She might be planning to leave tomorrow. Perhaps there were no lights on in the house because she'd gone to bed.'

Driving the short distance to the next village, Dan retraced the journey he'd made a few minutes previously.

When he got to Trudi's house for the second time that evening he walked up to the front door and rang the doorbell several times. After getting no response, he used a key that she'd given him to let himself in. He turned on the lights and shouted up the stairs. There was no reply. He bounded up the stairs two at a time, dreading what he might find. But the upstairs rooms were also empty.

He just couldn't think why she should act in such a bizarre way. He went back over recent events, turning over in his mind the last few hours to see if he could pinpoint what could have made her act so impetuously. Thinking back, it all seemed to stem from when Trudi had walked out of the clubhouse with that dark-haired girl, the one with the band.

Dan glanced at his watch. It was almost midnight, the time when the jazz evening was due to end. If he rushed back to the clubhouse he might just catch her…

All the way back, Dan relentlessly went over recent events in his mind, desperately searching for an answer, desperately trying to understand why she'd left him. Because that's what all this amounted to—Trudi had upped and left him a few weeks before they were going to be married. And he had absolutely no idea why.

As he drove into the car park at the yacht club he saw to his dismay that several people were already leaving. He parked hurriedly and sprinted into the clubhouse. To his relief the dark-haired girl was still there, helping the band pack up their equipment.

'Can we have another word?' he blurted out. 'I've got to speak to you, urgently.' Dan took her by the arm and tried to get her to move away a little from the musicians who were packing up.

She saw the thunderous look in his eyes and realised that something was amiss.

'Is is about Trudi?' she asked worriedly.

'Yes,' he replied. 'I don't know what's going on. I don't know where she is, but she went to pick up her daughter from my sister's house and left a message saying she was going away for a few days. Just like that! I'm very relieved that she hasn't entirely disappeared off the face of the earth, but I still have no idea where she is. I now realise that I know nothing about Trudi's past except that she has no family apart from her small daughter. I'm extremely worried about her and wondered if you could shed some light on where she might have gone. Did she, for instance, give any clue in the conversation you and she had? By the way, what is your name?'

'Annie.'

'Mine's Dan.'

Annie didn't know what to say. For a start, she had a sneaking feeling that Trudi hadn't told Dan the whole story about the surrogate pregnancy, and she didn't want to be the one to tell him. It was up to Trudi to tell him, if she wanted to.

'All I can say, Dan, is that she didn't tell me she was thinking of leaving, so I'm just as surprised as you to find her gone. Perhaps you should go to the police, you know, in case she's had some sort of breakdown.'

'Why should she have a breakdown? Has she had one before?'

'No.' She disappeared before, thought Annie, but I don't want to start getting into that. And she knew exactly what she was doing.

'Are you coming, Annie?' said one of the musicians. Everything was now packed up and they were ready to leave. The young man was eyeing Dan with suspicion. 'Everything sorted out, then?'

'Yes,' said Annie brightly. 'Everything's fine now and I'm ready to go.' She turned to Dan and said, 'I'm sure it's nothing to worry about. She'll turn up when she's ready…she always does.'

Dan looked startled.

'She's done this before, has she?'

Annie could have cursed herself. 'Only once.'

'I'm definitely calling the police,' decided Dan.

CHAPTER TEN

TRUDI drove into the night, on and on, with tears streaming down her face and no idea where she was going.

When she'd picked up Grace from Clare's she'd prepared a makeshift bed for her on the back seat of the car. The car boot had been filled with as much clothing and baby equipment as she'd been able to fit in. It had taken only minutes to do it once she'd been dropped home by the taxi.

Finally she'd written a letter to Dan and had posted it in the village on the way to Clare's. It had been a short letter, explaining about the surrogacy and how she'd found it difficult to tell him. And that she needed to get away for a few days to give them both some space and then, if he still felt the same about her, well, they could get married as planned. And if he didn't feel the same about her… That bit had been left unsaid, but she was sure he'd understand what she'd been trying to say. Then she'd driven the short distance to pick up Grace. And headed north.

After driving for a couple of hours, she pulled into a motorway service area and took out her road map. Her head was clearing a little and she'd stopped crying. The impulse which had caused her to take flight was now ebbing, enabling her to think more rationally. She was still intent on leaving for a while, but she was calmer and in a better frame of mind to decide exactly where she was going and what she might do in order to make yet another new start.

On the route map she traced the direction of the road she was on, the A1, and saw it was leading to Yorkshire. How ironic! But Yorkshire was a big place…

She moved her finger along the line of the A1 and looked for somewhere suitable to make her goal. She was prepared to drive through the night, just taking the occasional break, like she was doing now. She wasn't tired—she felt more awake than if she'd risen from a full night's sleep.

She checked the back seat.

'Where shall we go?' she whispered to the small slumbering figure. She looked with envious eyes at Grace, deep in blissful sleep, oblivious to the world and all its woes.

Back to the map, and her eye was caught by a familiar name. Chrishallthwaite. Now, where had she heard that before? According to the map it was a few miles past the town of Richmond in the Yorkshire Dales. It appeared to be in a valley at a point where two rivers met.

Then she remembered.

It had been Dan who'd told her about Chrishallthwaite. That was the village where his uncle used to live in a farm cottage. Heaven on earth, he'd called it. When he'd told her about the area she recalled how her spirits had soared and how she'd longed to go there. Well, now she could. At least she could give it a try. After all, she had nowhere else in mind…

'Like a couple of gypsies,' Trudi said to the softly breathing figure on the back seat, 'That's what we are.'

She started the engine. The thought of acting like a gypsy didn't depress her at all—just the opposite— and as she pulled onto the motorway again she found herself in a euphoric mood. She was even singing.

She drove on till daybreak, stopping occasionally to fill up with petrol or to check the route on the map. Grace woke with the sunrise and Trudi stopped at the next service station for breakfast and to freshen them both up. By the time they reached the pretty old market town of Richmond the rest of the world seemed to be waking up and going about its business.

With the skyline dominated by the ruins of a Norman castle, the town was like a gateway to the past. It seemed to be a place untouched by the modern world, with its large cobbled market-place, narrow streets and quaint old buildings.

She negotiated her way through the town and out on a road that followed the course of the River Swale—a beautiful, wide river abundantly endowed with cascades and waterfalls.

It was a glorious day and the sun sparkled on the swift-flowing water as she drove alongside the river through miles of beautiful countryside—by high moors, wooded banks and gentle valleys.

'No wonder Dan loved this place,' said Trudi to Grace, who was gurgling in her baby seat.

Stopping occasionally to consult the map, Trudi eventually found herself driving along a wooded valley road and into the small village of

Chrishallthwaite. She parked the car outside an attractive-looking pub called the Rose and Crown.

'Here we are, Grace. Our journey's end.'

Unstrapping the baby from her seat, Trudi carried her into the stone-built pub. Inside it was warm and welcoming and behind the bar was a rosy-faced woman who greeted them with a smile.

'Do you do bed and breakfast?' enquired Trudi, more in hope than expectation. The Rose and Crown had fine oak beams and an open fire but no B&B sign in evidence.

'We don't, dear,' said the landlady, looking regretful. 'There's a youth hostel through the village…but it's not really practical with a baby. I'm not sure if they do cots and that sort of thing. Was it just for the one night?'

'No. A few days was what I had in mind,' replied Trudi, showing her disappointment. Now that she'd found this idyllic little village she was desperately keen to stay here.

'In that case,' said the woman, 'there's a farm about half a mile away and they rent out holiday cottages. They used to be farm workers' houses but the Pattersons have turned them into very nice little holiday homes.'

Trudi's eyes lit up. 'That sounds wonderful! I do hope they've got one free.'

'I'll phone for you, shall I, dear?' The woman picked up the phone behind the bar and rang to enquire. 'Yes,' she said, cupping her hand over the handset, 'they've got one available right now. How long will you want it for?'

'A week, please,' said Trudi. She was due quite

a few days' leave and she hoped that Human Resources wouldn't have a problem with her taking them without giving any notice. They were usually understanding about family emergencies and, as far as Trudi was concerned, this was one. She planned to phone the hospital the next morning to sort it out.

The woman finished making the arrangements and gave Trudi directions. Trudi thanked her gratefully and set off to drive the short distance to the Pattersons' farm.

There were four self-catering cottages, each with its own small garden, built near to the large stone farmhouse.

'The farm workers used to grow their own vegetables and flowers,' explained Mrs Patterson, 'but for the holiday visitors we've put flagstones down to make a nice patio and barbecue area and a small piece of lawn. That's what holidaymakers seem to want these days.'

Trudi was delighted with the small cottage and felt very lucky to have got it for the week—especially as the other cottages were fully booked.

'I suppose it's because Chrishallthwaite is in such a gorgeous part of the country,' ventured Trudi when she was told that they were nearly always fully booked in the holiday season.

'That's true,' confirmed Mrs Patterson, 'and also the fact that we're near where they do the filming for quite a few TV series, *Home Farm* and *Den of the Dales* and that one about the flying vet. People love to go on "TV heritage" trips, half expecting to see their favourite soap characters walking around the place!'

'I never thought of that,' said Trudi, smiling at the small child standing next to his mother in the cosy farmhouse kitchen. Trudi had followed Mrs Patterson into the farmhouse to write her a cheque for the week's rent, and the woman had offered to hold the baby for a moment while she did so. The little boy, aged about six, Trudi estimated, was a Down's syndrome child.

'Is that your baby?' he asked Trudi.

'Yes.'

'What's her name?'

'She's called Grace. What's your name?'

'Andrew. Can I play with Grace?'

'He loves babies,' explained Mrs Patterson. 'In fact, he loves everybody.' She smiled indulgently at the little boy. 'Can I put the baby down on the carpet so that he can talk to her?'

'Of course,' said Trudi. She was touched by the way Andrew's eyes lit up when he heard her give permission. Grace, as usual, was delighted to see another child and the two of them played together happily for a few minutes.

'He doesn't get to play with many children,' said Andrew's mother. 'Unfortunately, he has a heart problem and so he isn't able to go to a special school—or any school for that matter. He's always thrilled when any children come here.'

'What a shame,' said Trudi, watching the gentle way the little boy played with the baby, not the usual rough-and-tumble way employed by most six-year-old boys.

'What kind of heart problem does he have?' Trudi, from her hospital experience, was aware that many Down's syndrome children suffered from heart problems—at Highfield they had a special clinic for their particular medical problems.

'We're not sure,' said Mrs Patterson. 'Andrew needs to be seen by a specialist, our doctor said. We're still waiting for an appointment. I'm afraid we can't afford to pay privately. My husband's a farmer and, contrary to what many people believe, we aren't rolling in money! In fact, without the rents coming in from the holiday cottages we'd be in big trouble—so there's no spare cash to pay privately for Andrew.'

'And you shouldn't have to,' said Trudi sympathetically, remembering how distraught she'd been when she'd been told that Grace might have a heart defect. Having medical connections, it had meant she'd been able to 'short cut' the system and get to see a cardiologist the next day, instead of spending weeks on a waiting list.

In a flashback she recalled that that had been the first time she'd set eyes on Dan. He'd been so calm and reassuring… And so breathtakingly attractive. Even though she'd been very concerned about Grace, she'd still managed to notice that!

She blinked hard to make the unbidden image fade from her mind.

She handed the cheque over and was given the cottage keys in return.

'All the linen is provided,' said Mrs Patterson, 'and if you need any provisions there's a well-stocked general store in the village. It had been closed for years, but with all the interest created by the TV series it opened up again. Before that, we had to drive ten miles to the nearest shop.'

'Have you seen me on TV?' asked Andrew, who had sidled up to Trudi. 'I'm on TV, I am.'

She looked at his mother for guidance, not wishing to deflate the small boy's ego.

'It's true.' Mrs Patterson laughed. 'Andrew has a small part in *Den of the Dales* and he's thrilled about it. All he has to do is sit next to the actor who's supposed to be his father and smile on cue.'

'That's wonderful!' said Trudi to Andrew. 'I never thought I'd be meeting someone *famous* when I came up to Yorkshire today!'

Andrew beamed with pride. 'Have you seen me on TV?'

'I haven't been watching *Den of the Dales* recently, but I certainly shall from now on!'

'I'll come and tell you when it's on, if you like,' Andrew offered enthusiastically.

His mother intervened. 'The lady won't want you bothering her when she's on holiday,' she said, adding under her breath to Trudi, 'I'll make sure he doesn't make a nuisance of himself. He tends to want to come round and play whenever there are children in the holiday cottages.'

'I don't mind at all, Mrs Patterson,' replied Trudi, totally captivated by the small boy. 'Andrew will be welcome at the cottage any time he likes. Grace will love having someone to play with—especially someone as famous as Andrew.'

Trudi unloaded the car and carried everything into the cottage, before driving back to the village to stock up on food and other essentials. She noted that there was a payphone outside the Rose and Crown, which she could use the next morning to phone the hospital.

Early on Monday, feeling the tension between her shoulder-blades, she dialled Highfield Hospital. She crossed her fingers, hoping there would be someone in the Human Resources department. Trudi relaxed when she was put through to the friendly voice of the Human Resources manager, a woman with whom she got on well.

Explaining how she needed to take a break, even though she'd given no notice, she said that she hoped it wouldn't cause too much of a problem.

'No problem at all,' said the manager. 'You have a good holiday. You deserve it—and you've got quite a lot of time owing to you. See you next week.'

Trudi breathed a sigh of relief as she replaced the receiver. She now had a whole week to get herself together, to work out a plan for the future.

She wondered if Dan had received her letter yet. It had been posted very late, so the chances were it would be the next day before he read her explanation. Her confession. A week would give him time to think about how he felt once he knew the truth about her. How would he react? Would it really be over between them? Would it make no difference or, once he'd had time to think things over, would he be glad that she'd released him from his commitment to marry her?

She could hardly bear to think about it…or him.

She had to drive slowly back to the farm cottage because her eyes were blurred with unshed tears.

'What do you mean, she's disappeared?' said Clare crossly. 'People just don't disappear.'

'Oh, yes, they do, and frequently, if you believe what the police have to say on the matter.' Dan was finding his sister's attitude deeply irritating. Trudi had vanished without trace and Clare was acting as if he was imagining the whole thing.

It had been nearly twenty-four hours since Trudi had last been seen and he'd spent virtually the whole of that time searching for her. He'd had no sleep and nothing to eat. Cups of black coffee had been all he'd been able to manage...all he'd been able to stomach. He'd driven back and forth between the yacht club, Trudi's house, his sister's house and his own flat in town, imagining that she might turn up at any one of them. He'd contacted the police, whom he'd found disappointingly unhelpful.

'How long has this lady been missing, sir?'

'Since about eleven last night.'

'Is she a minor?'

'No.'

'Do you suspect her of committing a crime?'

'Certainly not.'

'Is there any evidence of a crime being committed against her?'

'No.'

'Is she a relative?'

'Not yet. We're due to be married in six weeks.'

He found the half-smile that the desk sergeant gave him infuriating. He knew what the officer was thinking. That this was just a 'lovers' tiff' and that one of them was playing a game with the other. Very much the attitude his sister had taken.

'Well, sir, it isn't a crime for someone to go away on their own for a few hours…or a few days…or a few weeks for that matter. People do it all the time. We've hundreds of missing persons on our books. If it's any comfort to you, sir, most do turn up eventually, safe and sound.'

'No, it isn't any comfort to me, Officer,' said Dan, barely able to conceal his annoyance.

'I'll take the lady's details and we can set the paperwork in motion.'

The officer started filling in a form. Dan answered all his questions, giving as much information as he could about Trudi and Grace.

'We've got quite a bit to go on here, sir—descriptions, car registration. We'll put it out on the missing persons search list. Don't forget to contact us straight away if the lady turns up—as I'm sure she will. You wouldn't want to get accused of wasting police time, would you?'

This last remark was spoken in a light-hearted manner but in Dan's sleep-starved state of mind it made him want to pick up the form, roll it up and insert it down the police officer's throat.

Restraining the impulse, he turned and walked out of the police station. Then he drove once again to his sister's—purely because he couldn't think of what else to do.

He was beginning to regret the decision because he couldn't persuade Clare that Trudi had definitely disappeared.

'She's probably just gone off for a little break on her own,' suggested his sister. 'Perhaps you were become a little too demanding.'

'What are you talking about? What do you mean, *demanding*?'

Clare gave him a sultry look under lowered eyelashes.

'I know what you men are like,' she said huskily. 'A sex-starved, red-blooded male like you probably went berserk when you and she finally got it together. Know what I mean?'

She winked at him.

He was infuriated! The woman he loved had gone—heaven knew where—and all his sister could do was make crude jokes.

'If that's all you have to say then I'm off!'

He stood up, knocking over the kitchen chair as he made for the door.

Realising she'd gone too far, Clare stood in the doorway, blocking it with her outstretched arms.

'Dan, I'm sorry. I just wanted to make you lighten up a little. You're getting yourself in a terrible state.'

Dan moved her arms out of the way and walked to the door. 'Well, there's no point in me staying here any longer. I need to get some sleep or I'll be useless at the hospital tomorrow.'

'You are going in to work tomorrow, are you?' asked his sister in subdued tones.

'Yes. There's nothing else I can do as far as Trudi is concerned. Anyway, she might turn up at the hospital.' Dan cheered himself up with this thought.

'That's right,' said Clare, putting on a reassuring

smile for his benefit. 'She'll turn up at the hospital, as right as rain.'

Closing the front door behind Dan, she leaned on it and let her false smile drop.

'I hope to God she does!'

CHAPTER ELEVEN

'OF COURSE I can cope without you,' replied Stuart Walker, Dan's registrar. 'It'll be my big opportunity to pose around and pretend I'm a consultant.'

Dan laughed for the first time that morning. Stuart's irreverent remarks might have gained him minus points with some of the older specialists who took themselves and their status very seriously, but Dan found Stuart a real tonic. His subversive humour regularly livened up the more mundane working hours or helped them all to cope with some of the sadder days when the news was particularly bad for one of their young patients.

'You're like a wet blanket today,' remarked Stuart after they'd completed the morning clinic and Dan had explained what had happened. 'Taking the rest of the week off to try and find Trudi is the most sensible suggestion you've made so far.'

They'd been walking to the canteen when Dan had asked his registrar if he could take over for a short while, hopefully just to the end of the week.

This morning he'd arrived early at the hospital buoyed up by the hope that he'd find his fiancée working in the outpatients department as usual. His disappointment when he'd found she hadn't been there, that she'd phoned in to say she was taking a week's holiday, had sent his spirits spiralling downwards.

'I'll just have a coffee,' he said in answer to Stuart's enquiry about food.

'I think a good plate of hospital canteen pasta will do you a power of good. You look as if you're in training for a part in a horror movie—you know, one of those guys who've been chained up in a dark dungeon for twenty years and fed on bread and water, if they were lucky.'

Dan gave in gracefully and managed to eat a surprisingly large portion.

'Have you any idea where to start looking for her?' enquired Stuart who was now tucking into a dish of jam sponge and custard.

'Not really,' admitted Dan. 'But I've got to do something, look somewhere. I was so convinced that she'd turn up at work today that I'd put all other ideas of where to search for her to the back of my mind. The trouble, I now realise, is that I know so little about her. Where she comes from, who her friends are…that kind of thing.'

'You mentioned someone called Annie,' prompted Stuart. 'Could she help?'

'Perhaps,' conceded Dan. 'She's someone I'll certainly get in touch with again. I don't know where she lives but I do know that she works at Mayside General.'

'Go *now*,' said Stuart. 'Drive there this afternoon and then at least you'll feel you're doing something. And who knows? You might strike lucky first time. She might have moved in with this Annie for a week's holiday.'

'Mmm.' Dan wasn't convinced of that, but Annie might give him a few leads, fill him in on some of

Trudi's 'missing' years and give him a clue to where she might be now.

Annie recognised Dan immediately when he walked into her ward. But he was looking more distressed than when she'd seen him before...he'd obviously been going through hell.

'I hope you don't mind me barging in like this,' he said.

He seemed a different person—a broken man. Her heart went out to him and she smiled at him in her friendliest manner—the kind of smile she reserved for seriously ill patients.

'Fancy seeing you again!' she said. 'Any news of Trudi?' Of course, she knew what the answer would be just by looking at him, but she imagined it would help matters if she brought up the subject first.

As she'd expected, he shook his head. 'That's why I've come to speak to you, Annie. Can you spare a few minutes?'

'I'm just going for a break,' she said. 'Come along and we can talk over a cuppa.'

Sitting in a quiet corner, they talked about Trudi. Dan learned things about her he'd never known— where she used to live, the names of her sister and brother-in-law, how her sister, Jane, had been trying to conceive for years and eventually had had to have a hysterectomy at a relatively young age... And many other small details which he jotted down in case they proved to be significant in his search for her.

'Can you think of *anywhere* she might have

gone?' Dan asked. 'Somewhere she might have mentioned as being the ideal spot she'd run away to?'

Annie shook her head.

'We never talked about things like that. It was more boyfriend trouble and that kind of thing. You know, girl talk. There was a bloke who conned her out of a lot of money and she was furious at being taken in by him. I do remember that. But she never spoke about some special hide-away or anything like that.'

'A hide-away,' repeated Dan. 'Yes, that's the kind of place…'

The words sounded familiar he could even hear Trudi saying them. What had she said when they'd been out sailing just over a week ago? 'A place where you could lose all your troubles…an ideal hide-away…' They'd been talking about the little Yorkshire village he stayed in as a boy. Chrishallthwaite…where his uncle had had a farm cottage. She'd asked him about the place and her face had gone all dreamy as he'd described it.

'Are you OK?' asked Annie. 'You've gone even paler than you were before.'

He shook himself from his daydream.

'I think I might have answered my own question,' he said. 'There's a place she might have gone. It's an outside chance but, then, everything is when you've nothing to go on. Clutching at straws seems to be the only sensible thing to do right now.'

After Dan left Annie at Mayside, he drove to one of the addresses she'd given him, the place where Trudi had lived.

It was a large house, turned into four flats, and he knew he was wasting his time even as he pushed the first doorbell. The occupant, a young man with a ponytail and an abundance of facial piercings, turned out to be very articulate and well spoken. He listened to Dan's enquiries and said that no one of Trudi's description had been near the apartments in recent days.

'I'm very observant,' he said pleasantly. 'I'm doing a law degree and plan to get a job with the CID, so I keep my eyes peeled in training, so to speak.'

Dan drove around to several other addresses given him by Annie—addresses of some of Trudi's friends and acquaintances—but none of them had heard from her for a long time.

The more he thought about it, the more convinced he was that she'd just set off in the car that night with no particular place in mind…and that she might just have considered driving to the small village in Yorkshire which she'd said would make an ideal hide-away.

It was getting dark but Dan decided he'd set off straight away. He could break his journey in a motel if he got tired, but right now he needed to get moving, get on the road to where Trudi might be.

A quick glance at the map and within minutes he was heading north—to Yorkshire.

Despite being in a strange environment, Grace had taken the upheaval of leaving home and her familiar surroundings with a pinch of salt.

Even Trudi, after two days in the peaceful Yorkshire countryside, was beginning to calm down and be her old self again. A holiday what just what she needed.

She was sitting, just staring out of the back window at the peaceful country scene outside, when there was a knock at the door. She peered through the front window and saw that it was Mrs Patterson and Andrew.

'Come in,' she said, opening the door to them.

'We won't stop for long,' said Mrs Patterson, 'because we're out doing some filming. Well, Andrew is, for *Den of the Dales*.'

'How exciting!' said Trudi to the little boy.

'We were wondering if you, or rather Grace, fancied being a TV star as well?' ventured Mrs Patterson. 'The director is looking for a baby of about Grace's age to play a small part. One of the characters, it might even be ''Den'' himself, is going to be confronted by an old girlfriend with a baby— and it may or may not turn out to be his child. You know the kind of thing—a typical soap-opera theme! The baby they'd cast in the part has got a bad cold and her mother phoned the film crew this morning to call it off. The director's going mad, trying to find a replacement baby. Then I thought about yours.'

Trudi looked down at the rug where Grace was playing happily with Andrew.

'Well, yes…that would be great,' she answered, slightly unsettled by this unexpected request. 'She won't be able to make many appearances, though, because we're only here for a few more days.'

'It's only going to be for this one episode,' Mrs Patterson assured her. 'Even if she does turn out to be Den's baby—I'm speaking as if the characters are real people, but you know what I mean—the girl-friend is going back to Australia with the child. I read that much in the script, so I wouldn't worry about any long-term commitment. And you'll get paid for it, of course.'

· 'When do they want us?' asked Trudi.

'As soon as you can get there. If you follow us in the car I'll show you the way. It's up an old farm track—they're filming up the hill near the ruins of an old lead mine and smelt mill. Sounds dreadful but it really is a beautiful setting—there's a little stream and an old stone bridge and open moorland. Just make sure that you and Grace are wrapped up well in your thickest jumpers and anoraks…there's a lot of hanging about and it can get quite cold. It's not glamorous at all. You wait for ages to do your bit and then they have to film it from several angles over and over again. But that's show biz for you!'

Following closely behind the Pattersons' four-wheel drive, Trudi was convinced her exhaust pipe was going to get knocked off by the large bumps and humps that dotted the rutted farm track leading to the filming site.

After driving for a mile or so, they turned a bend and all the paraphernalia of the *Den of the Dales* film crew was revealed to them. Trudi's stomach went into a tight knot as she anticipated the exciting, un-real world of film and television that she was going to be part of for that one day.

Mrs Patterson—'Call me Josie'—introduced her to the director, who was only really interested in the baby.

'Fabulous,' he said, giving Grace the once-over. 'Fabulous baby.'

'Thanks,' said Trudi proudly.

'What's her name?'

'Grace.'

'Fabulous,' repeated the director. 'Bev, my production assistant, will take you over and introduce you and Grace to Gary Lawson. Gary, as I'm sure you know, plays ''Den'' of the Dales.'

The director waved over a blonde girl with a clipboard.

'This is Trudi and her baby, Grace, whose playing Den's illegitimate kid.'

'Fabulous,' said Bev.

'I'm going to change the name of the baby in the script to Grace,' he said to Trudi. 'She might respond better if she hears her own name, don't you think?'

'Oh, yes,' agreed Trudi, impressed by all the activity going on around her...cameramen and sound recordists and boom-holders bobbing about all over the place...actors milling around, some having paint and powder put on by make-up artists...a food wagon serving coffee, tea and bacon sandwiches to all comers...and a large van which, from the sound of it, contained a generator.

'Bev, take Trudi and Grace over to meet Gary,' instructed the director. 'She might as well get used to being held by her new ''daddy''. Only in the story, of course!'

'Fabulous,' said Trudi, catching on to the lingo.

'Spoken like a real pro,' Josie Patterson said with a giggle when the director was out of earshot. 'It's all quite fun, really.'

'I can imagine,' agreed Trudi, entering into the spirit of things. It was only going to be for one day so she might as well throw herself into it whole-heartedly!

She was introduced to an actor whom she now recognised from TV. She wasn't a great fan of this particular daytime soap, but she'd seen it occasionally and as she looked around she noticed one or two familiar 'famous' faces.

'So this is my little girl!' said Gary 'Den of the Dales' Lawson. He took Grace in his arms and she gurgled with delight.

'What a trouper!' exclaimed Gary. 'I can see a bright future in the acting business for this little lady.'

Trudi breathed a sigh of relief. Thank goodness Grace wasn't having one of her rare 'off' days when she only wanted to be held by her. Those days were few and far between, but they did happen and it would have been most embarrassing if this had turned out to be one of them!

They rehearsed and filmed all morning. Trudi and Josie were given ringside seats so they could watch their 'actor' children performing.

'I don't know if I could take this lifestyle full time,' said Josie, 'but it's quite fun now and again.'

'It certainly is,' agreed Trudi as she waved at Grace who was at that moment being carried by an actress with an Australian accent.

'I'm sure I've seen that girl before,' she remarked.

'She's a big star in one of the Aussie soaps,' said Josie.

'Ah! She might be a big star but she doesn't know

how to hold a baby. She's holding Grace as if she were a sack of potatoes!'

The two women laughed. Andrew, who'd finished doing his scenes, came over to join them.

'You were very good,' said his mother. 'What did the director say?'

'He said I was fabulous,' said Andrew proudly.

As the afternoon wore on and the light began to fade, the director called it a day.

'That's it, everyone. It's a wrap.'

Carrying Grace, he strolled over to where the two women were sitting.

'This little one has been so good,' he told Trudi. 'Not a tear, not a whimper, just gurgles all the way. Pity we're only having her in the one episode.'

He handed Grace back to her mother.

'We're all going back to the Rose and Crown before we leave. Would you like to join us? Children are very welcome in the pub, I believe.'

'Yes, we'd love to,' said Trudi.

'We'd better get back,' said Josie. 'My husband will be coming in from the fields soon and I've got to get the meal on. But you go, Trudi. You're on holiday after all.'

CHAPTER TWELVE

Dan drove into Chrishallthwaite in the late afternoon sunshine. It was as he remembered it from his childhood, stone buildings straggling along the one main street, with a backdrop of craggy hills and the sparkling torrent of the River Swale sweeping under an old iron bridge.

He stopped his car outside the old chapel and looked around. The streets were deserted. He was disappointed that there was no one around to speak to, to ask…what? Yes, what precisely was he going to ask the first inhabitant of Chrishallthwaite that he bumped into?

On second thought, perhaps coming here hadn't been such a good idea after all. He was searching for a needle in a haystack…but he wasn't going to let that depress him. Being back in his favourite childhood place was having a soothing effect on him and he started to hum to himself. He could do worse than stay here overnight—there was a youth hostel, he recalled. Roughing it for a night or two wouldn't do him any harm, he decided, and it probably wouldn't be much worse than the grim motel he'd stayed in the previous night. Anyway, he wasn't looking his best, wearing yesterday's shirt and having had a most unsatisfactory shave with a lady's disposable razor which had been all the motel had provided in the bathroom. Thank heavens he'd been able to buy a toothbrush as well or he'd have felt completely disgusting as opposed to only fairly disgusting. So who was he to start being fussy about sleeping in a youth hostel?

He started the engine and drove slowly through the village.

'At least there's some life here,' he muttered, seeing several cars parked outside the Rose and Crown.

He had a yen to try and find the farm cottage where his uncle had once lived. Driving past the youth hostel sign, he carried on for about half a mile and came to a farm. He was convinced this was where his uncle had worked. The line of workers' cottages looked familiar and as he drove into the yard he was transported back nearly thirty years. He noticed a sign saying HOLIDAY COTTAGES TO RENT and couldn't help giving a hollow laugh.

'Holiday cottages! And here was I thinking nothing had changed.'

A woman and a small boy came over to him. He rolled down the window. He noticed that the boy was a Down's syndrome child. Automatically, he smiled at him and said, 'Hi. How are you doing?'

'Fabulous,' said Andrew, his eyes bright with enthusiasm.

'I'm sorry but we're fully booked,' said his mother.

'What a shame,' replied Dan. 'I used to come here as a child. My uncle lived here. It brings back many happy memories.'

'We might have a cottage available next week,' she offered.

'Don't worry. I was only passing through. I hadn't

really decided to stay for that long, just one night at most. I'm just going back into the village to have another look around for old times' sake.'

As he was speaking to the farmer's wife he was casting his eyes over the cars parked outside the holiday cottages. Trudi's car wasn't one of them—and he could hardly go peering in the windows like a peeping Tom. You got arrested for that kind of thing!

'I know this sounds silly,' he ventured, 'but I'm looking for someone and I wondered if she might be here. She's got medium-length auburn hair and she has a baby aged about one year. I've been looking high and low for her.'

Mrs Patterson bent down to Andrew and told him to run inside because it was getting cold. As the boy ran off she straightened up, her face in a fixed expression.

'You may have come here as a child, but now you're a stranger and I'm not telling you anything about anyone.'

Dan was dismayed to see that the woman's friendly attitude had now changed to one of deep suspicion.

'If your lady doesn't want to be found, then she doesn't want to be found,' she continued grimly. 'I don't know who you are but if you don't leave my land I'm going to call my husband and he'll sort out your nice car with his big tractor.'

Dan knew he was going to get nowhere with this extremely protective woman, but her knee-jerk reaction to his innocent enquiry gave him hope that maybe she was shielding someone—an auburn-haired woman with a baby, perhaps?

He closed the car window, restarted the car and drove away, heading back into the village. That strange encounter had left a bitter taste in his mouth and he decided that what he really needed now was a pint of local beer.

He found one of the last places in the Rose and Crown car park and locked his car.

He was walking into the pub when he did a double-take. There, among the many vehicles of varying shapes and sizes, was a red hatchback with a familiar number plate. He went over to it, barely able to believe his eyes. The numbers were swimming in his vision and he held his breath, hardly daring to hope it might be Trudi's. It could, after all, be an identical car with an almost identical number plate.

He peered into the back and saw the baby seat and next to it a small navy jacket with a daisy motif. He'd been with Trudi when she'd bought it for Grace. 'Navy's good,' she'd told him. 'Goes with anything and doesn't show every tiny mark.'

His hand was shaking as he pushed open the pub door. Inside, the main bar was very busy, with the landlady taking orders and despatching drinks to the noisy, good-natured, jostling group who appeared to be in high spirits. He stood still for a few moments and let his eyes act like searchlights, scanning the large room with all its alcoves and corners.

Then he saw her.

Trudi was sitting with her back to him in a group of people, one of whom was holding Grace. Dan moved with bated breath over towards her. A man, a good-looking type, was holding Grace as she jumped up and down on his knee, whooping with delight.

'Who's my little girl, then?' he kept saying. 'Say ''Daddy''. Can you say that, Grace? Daddy. Daddy.' And when Grace did as she was bidden, saying 'Dadda', everyone at the table clapped delightedly— including Trudi!

Dan was dumbstruck. Who was this man? Could he possibly be Grace's real father? Had he come all this way, spent days in agony wondering where she'd gone, only to find she'd run away to be with someone else?

He felt sick.

The man who was playing with Grace caught his eye and noticed the look on his face. He said something to Trudi which Dan overheard—something about the Grim Reaper watching them.

She turned and saw Dan. Her face was a picture. She didn't know whether to laugh or cry. Instead, she leapt up, nearly knocking over her wineglass, and rushed across to him, flinging her arms around him.

'Dan!' she gasped, burying her head in his chest. His arms closed around her.

'Oh, my love.' It was all he could say as he hugged her slim form to him, never wanting to let her go.

'You got my letter, and you still came!' She was crying into his shoulder, unable to stop herself.

'What letter? There was no letter.'

Trudi pulled away and looked into his eyes, and the dark shadows under them. 'But I posted it to you, explaining that I needed to get away for a few days…and to let you have time to think about the surrogacy thing.'

'I haven't been home for a couple of days,' said Dan, 'I've been racing round the country, trying to find you!' He paused, having just taken in what she'd said. 'Surrogacy? What surrogacy?'

Trudi dropped her arms down by her side and stared at the floor. So he didn't know. And she'd believed that he'd read her letter and he'd still come to find her, when in truth he didn't know the half of it! She couldn't hide the disappointment in her voice.

'Oh, Dan. I thought you knew.'

'Knew what?'

She led him to a quiet corner of the room where they weren't in danger of being overheard by the others.

'Grace was a surrogate baby,' she started haltingly. She saw Dan's eyebrows shoot up, but she pressed on. 'I offered to have a baby for my sister, Jane, and her husband, Rob. They were unable to have children, having tried all the fertility treatments available. And then, on top of everything, Jane was told she had to have a hysterectomy. She was completely devastated and I'm sure she was on the verge of suicide. So I said I'd do it. Have a baby for her. You see, Jane and I had been through such tough times when we were kids—we were really close. So when she couldn't have a baby it seemed the most natural thing in the world that I should have one for her.'

Dan was hanging on her every word. 'What happened to Jane?' he asked. 'Why didn't you give Grace to her like you promised?'

Trudi gulped. 'She and Rob were killed in a car crash on the day Grace was born.'

'Oh, God,' said Dan. He put his arms around her and felt her trembling. 'You poor angel, how terrible…how terrible.'

'That's why I kept the baby,' she said, weeping softly. 'And the awful thing is, I was glad that I was able to keep her because I'm sure I would never have been able to give her away.'

'But, darling,' said Dan gently, brushing her tears from her cheek with the flat of his hand, 'why didn't you tell me all this before? Didn't you think I'd understand?'

'I was going to,' she said. 'But then you started to tell me about Jasmine, and how you refused to give her a baby…and I thought you'd be very shocked to find out that I'd planned to give my sister a baby—to be a surrogate mother.'

'That was completely different!' he said. 'That woman was selfish and self-centred in the extreme—she just wanted to use me, and then cast me aside like an old glove. What you did for your sister was totally motivated by kindness and generosity.'

'Oh, Dan,' she said in utter relief, 'so you don't mind?'

'Mind? If anything, it makes me love you more.' His voice was low and husky. He pulled her closer and kissed her, tenderly at first, then with a desperate urgency.

'I thought I'd lost you,' he whispered hoarsely.

'And I thought I'd lost you,' she replied as his mouth came down on hers again. Oblivious to the fascinated stares of cast from *Den of the Dales*, they kissed long and deeply and hungrily.

A spontaneous burst of applause brought them back to earth. They looked up and saw eager faces looking their way. Trudi grinned.

'We're making quite an exhibition of ourselves, aren't we?' said Dan, joining in the laughter.

'By the way,' he said, a small prickle of concern in his voice, 'who's is that man holding Grace? I could have sworn I heard her call him Daddy. Is there something else you should be telling me? Is he her real father?'

Trudi guffawed at the very idea!

'He's Gary Lawson,' explained Trudi. 'You know, Den of *Den of the Dales*, the TV series. We've been doing some filming and Grace was playing his daughter. Let's go and join them,' she said to Dan. 'I'll explain all about it. Grace is going to be a TV star!'

'So you've forgiven me?' asked Trudi when the two of them were facing each other over a candlelit dinner in the cottage, a meal hastily prepared from the contents of a variety of tins and heated up on the cooker in the small kitchen.

'I've forgiven you but I'm not ever likely to forget this disappearing act of yours.' He clinked his wineglass to hers.

'I won't do it again, I promise.' She got up from the table and went over to him, settling herself comfortably on his knee. His arms folded around her, safely and securely. He kissed her and she snuggled up to him.

'I'm so lucky to have you,' she said. 'I'd got my-self into such an emotional state. Carrying a baby that I'd grown to love, all the time believing that I'd have to give it away when it was born… And then all the trauma of my sister's death, which brought on terrible guilt. Guilt because I was desperately sad that she'd died…but I was also relieved to know that, as a result of her death, I could keep the baby. I was just so mixed up. That kind of emotional upheaval makes you act in strange ways.'

'Like running away.'

'Yes. But not any more. The only place I want to be is with you.'

Early next morning, Trudi took Dan across to meet Josie Patterson to reassure her that she wasn't being stalked or anything sinister like that.

'We're getting married in five weeks,' she said. 'Dan's a paediatric cardiologist and I was telling him about Andrew and his heart problem and that he'd been waiting a long time to see a consultant. Dan says that he'd like to help out if he can and get things moving along for you.'

Josie Patterson's face creased into a smile. 'Would you? Would you really? We're so worried about Andrew in case he has something really serious wrong with his heart, and…' She couldn't finish the sentence. It was her ever-present fear that Andrew would die in his sleep or drop dead while playing or running around.

Dan handed her his card. 'Just ask your doctor to phone my secretary. She'll fix an appointment for you to see me professionally, and if there's anything that needs to be done I'll arrange for a cardiac surgeon to operate as quickly as possible.'

They stayed on in Chrishallthwaite until the end of the week. Dan took Trudi and Grace to all the places he'd loved so much in his boyhood.

Five weeks later they were married and Annie was a bridesmaid.

As they drove away on their honeymoon, Dan said, 'I've been thinking.'

'Oh?'

'I had to phone the police station to say that I'd found you, and the police officer made a very helpful suggestion.'

'Yes?'

'He offered to let me have one of those electronic tags. You could wear one, he said, and then I'd know exactly where to find you next time you disappeared!'

Trudi giggled, knowing she'd brought this on herself.

'How long is it going to be before I live this down? Before you'll happily let me out of your sight?'

Dan pretended to give the matter deep thought.

'The rest of our lives, I would think. Yes, that sounds about right to me.'

MILLS & BOON®

Makes any time special™

**Mills & Boon publish 29 new titles
every month. Select from...**

Modern Romance™   Tender Romance™

Sensual Romance™

Medical Romance™ Historical Romance™

MAT2

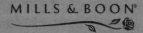

MILLS & BOON®

Medical Romance™

RESCUING DR RYAN *by Caroline Anderson*

Dr Will Ryan was supposed to be training the beautiful
Dr Lucie Compton but having injured himself in a fall he
now finds that he is totally dependent upon her for
help. Forced into constant contact they drive each
other crazy—in more ways than one...

FOUND: ONE HUSBAND *by Meredith Webber*

Out in the Australian rainforest an injured man literally
drops into nurse Sam Abbott's life. Getting him back to
safety was one problem, dealing with his amnesia was
going to present many more. All he could remember
was some medical knowledge. Was he a doctor? All
Sam knew was that her attraction for this intriguing
stranger with a wedding ring was about to lead her into
unknown territory!

A WIFE FOR DR CUNNINGHAM *by Maggie Kingsley*

Junior doctor Hannah Blake knows she can prove her
value to the A&E team at St Stephen's but her
relationship with the workaholic Dr Robert
Cunningham could be her undoing. He might accept her
as a colleague, even as a lover—but will he ever see her
as a wife?

On sale 6th April 2001

*Available at most branches of WH Smith, Tesco,
Martins, Borders, Easons, Volume One/James Thin
and most good paperback bookshops* 0301/03a

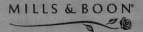

MILLS & BOON®

Medical Romance™

RELUCTANT PARTNERS *by Margaret Barker*

When the man who Dr Jane Crowther believes stood her up all those years ago joins her practice she is determined not to fall for his charms again. But GP Richard has no recollection of their date and sets about trying to unravel the past and to win Jane's love...

THE MIDWIFE'S CHILD *by Sarah Morgan*

Not wanting to force Jed Matthews into marriage midwife Brooke Daniels had fled after their night of passion together six years ago. Now he's back in her life and very interested in getting back in her bed but she has a secret that will change their lives forever...

SARA'S SECRET *by Anne Herries*

When Sister Sara and surgeon Richard Dalton meet there is instant chemistry between them. But with both of them traumatised by experiences in the past how can they ever overcome their fears and find love together?

On sale 6th April 2001

Available at most branches of WH Smith, Tesco, Martins, Borders, Easons, Volume One/James Thin and most good paperback bookshops 0301/03b

FREE

4 BOOKS
AND A SURPRISE GIFT!

We would like to take this opportunity to thank you for reading this Mills & Boon® book by offering you the chance to take FOUR more specially selected titles from the Medical Romance™ series absolutely FREE! We're also making this offer to introduce you to the benefits of the Reader Service™ —

★ FREE home delivery
★ FREE monthly Newsletter
★ FREE gifts and competitions
★ Exclusive Reader Service discounts
★ Books available before they're in the shops

Accepting these FREE books and gift places you under no obligation to buy; you may cancel at any time, even after receiving your free shipment. Simply complete your details below and return the entire page to the address below. *You don't even need a stamp!*

YES! Please send me 4 free Medical Romance books and a surprise gift. I understand that unless you hear from me, I will receive 6 superb new titles every month for just £2.49 each, postage and packing free. I am under no obligation to purchase any books and may cancel my subscription at any time. The free books and gift will be mine to keep in any case.

MIZEC

Ms/Mrs/Miss/Mr ....Initials ....
BLOCK CAPITALS PLEASE

Surname ....

Address ....

....

....Postcode ....

Send this whole page to:
UK: FREEPOST CN81, Croydon, CR9 3WZ
EIRE: PO Box 4546, Kilcock, County Kildare (stamp required)

Offer valid in UK and Eire only and not available to current Reader Service subscribers to this series. We reserve the right to refuse an application and applicants must be aged 18 years or over. Only one application per household. Terms and prices subject to change without notice. Offer expires 30th September 2001. As a result of this application, you may receive further offers from Harlequin Mills & Boon Limited and other carefully selected companies. If you would prefer not to share in this opportunity please write to The Data Manager at the address above.

Mills & Boon® is a registered trademark owned by Harlequin Mills & Boon Limited.
Medical Romance™ is being used as a trademark.